Party

I stared at the phone. *Lila* invited *Roary* to *my* party?

"In fact, I've invited a bunch of people. I told Roary to bring some of his friends."

Roary's friends! Roary's friends as in . . . high-school guys? What was Steven going to say? I'd told him it was just girls!

"Jessica? Are you there?"

"I'm here," I said quickly.

"It's okay that I invited them, isn't it?"

"Oh, sure," I said. My whole body had gone numb. I don't know why I felt like it would be impossible to tell Lila not to bring Roary and his friends. I just couldn't do it somehow. I didn't want her to think I'd gotten less cool than I used to be.

"I just thought that with no parents around, who's going to mind?" Lila explained. "Not Steven. I mean, some of these guys are his friends too."

"Oh, absolutely," I agreed, my mind racing. Lila was right. How could Steven get mad about guys coming over when the guys were friends of his?

"Besides," she went on, "some of them are really *cute*. You should be thanking me, Jessica."

I giggled. Cute guys—now that was an argument I understood. Wow. This party was going to be even cooler than I thought!

The Cool Crowd

Written by
Jamie Suzanne

Created by
FRANCINE PASCAL

BANTAM BOOKS
NEW YORK · TORONTO · LONDON · SYDNEY · AUCKLAND

RL 4, 008-012

THE COOL CROWD
A Bantam Book / May 1999

*Sweet Valley Junior High is a trademark of
Francine Pascal.*

Conceived by Francine Pascal.

*Produced by 17th Street Productions,
a division of Daniel Weiss Associates, Inc.
33 West 17th Street, New York, NY 10011.*

ISBN: 0-553-48663-2

Published simultaneously in the United States and Canada

PRINTED IN THE UNITED STATES OF AMERICA

OPM   0 9 8 7 6 5 4 3

To Mia Pascal Johansson

Jessica

"Ouch! Shoot!" I said as I accidentally slammed my finger in my locker. I jammed my pinky into my mouth, then pulled it out and inspected the damage. My locker door rattled loudly. I kicked it. Revenge is sweet.

"You okay?" Bethel McCoy asked, looking at my red finger. She grimaced and flashed me a sympathetic look.

"Yeah," I told her, blowing on my finger. Someone told me once that's supposed to make an injury feel better. Guess what? It totally doesn't work. "I don't have time to feel the pain anyway."

We were in the locker room after cross-country practice, and I was rushing to make the special bus that took home the kids on sports teams. I bent to pick up my bag, flipped my damp hair over my shoulder, and turned to go. "See you, Bethel."

"Hold up," she said. She pointed to a disgusting lump on one of the changing benches.

Jessica

"Don't forget your lucky sweat socks." Bethel grinned.

I rolled my eyes. "Thanks *so* much for reminding me," I said sarcastically. I picked up the socks between my index finger and thumb. Gross upon gross—they had actually been sitting there since *yesterday*. I unzipped my bag and shoved them in.

"And Jessica," Bethel said before I could sprint off again, "good run today."

She was putting something in her locker when she said it, so she didn't see my smile. It was just as well. I didn't want Bethel to think I was a total dork, grinning like a fool. But I couldn't help feeling pleased. Bethel's the best runner on the cross-country team—by *far*—and I had almost beaten her today.

"It wasn't as good as tomorrow's will be," I told her. "You better watch out, or you'll be eatin' my dust soon."

Bethel snorted and pretended she was about to toss her sweatshirt at my head. "Get out of here!"

I bolted for the door, laughing. "See you!"

"Bye!" she called. Her voice echoed through the locker room and faded as I burst out the door into the bright sunlight and bolted for my bus. I slipped into my seat just as the doors were closing. I was still smiling, thinking about the compliment Bethel gave me. She and I had started out not liking each other when I joined the team. But we'd gotten used to each other and were now even becoming friends.

I think. Bethel is kind of hard to read.

But still, I liked her. And it was really nice of her to say that I had run well. In fact, it made me grin to myself all the way to my bus stop. I got off the bus and started down the street toward a nice, hot shower and clothes that weren't wilted with sweat.

This was officially a very good day. In spite of my finger.

"Jessica! Wait!" called a familiar voice.

I whirled around to see Lila Fowler, my best friend. Or rather, she had been my best friend until I moved to a new school and my entire life had fallen apart. "Lila!" I was suddenly overwhelmed with the kind of feeling usually reserved for Christmas morning and my birthday—as in, total *joy.*

Lila trotted toward me, looking like she stepped right out of a fashion magazine. Her long, brown hair bounced and gleamed in the sun. I was suddenly aware of just how gross I looked, and I didn't even want to think about how I *smelled.* The Jessica Wakefield that Lila knew would never have walked around looking like such a slob.

Why do I have to run into her now? I'd worn cool flared jeans and a fitted top to school and had looked suitably glam practically all day. But for track practice I'd changed into an old T-shirt and spandex. Then I ran for two hours. Since I knew I was going right home after, I hadn't bothered to shower or change.

As Lila got closer, her smile faltered. She peered at me over the top of her designer sunglasses. "Nobody told me grunge was back."

"It pays to keep up with the trends," I said. "That showered look is *so* five minutes ago." Lila looked confused, so I smiled and shook my head. "I'm just *kidding*, Lila. Actually, I just got back from track practice."

"You . . . *what?*" Lila asked, as if I had just told her I was from Mars or joining the navy or something.

Lila and I went to the same school up until this year. Then they rezoned the district and my twin, Elizabeth, and I had been assigned to Sweet Valley Junior High while Lila and almost all my old friends stayed at Sweet Valley Middle School.

Back at Sweet Valley Middle, I'd been part of the It crowd. My friends were all the popular girls around school.

But that was history now. I had hardly any friends at my new school, although I was working on it. Today, for example, I had a real conversation with Kristin Seltzer, one of the most popular girls at SVJH. And there was Bethel, of course. Still, I was hardly part of the It crowd there.

"Track is cool at Sweet Valley Junior High," I said to Lila.

"Really?" Her eyes were wide.

"Of course," I insisted. It was cool with *me* anyway. "Why would I do it if it weren't cool?"

"Good point," Lila said. "SVJH sounds so weird! I'm glad I'm not there—I could never find the time to be on a track team," she went on. "There are so many parties to go to! You wouldn't believe how much clothing I've needed this year."

I hadn't been to *any* parties this year. I felt a pang. I hated to admit how much I missed my old life. My old friends.

"How are Mandy and Rachel?" I asked, eager to hear every detail. "What's Ellen up to?"

Lila shrugged. "Everybody is so busy, we hardly have time to talk on the phone." She and I fell into step toward home. "Mandy is dating this really cute guy, Chet, so that takes up a lot of her time. Rachel is in charge of planning all the parties at school. And Ellen has, like, five guys calling her all the time."

"Really?" I asked. *But Ellen was always such a klutz!* I wanted to say. Why did she get to be Little Miss Popularity while I had to sit around Friday nights watching movies with my parents?

"Really," Lila said with a little smile. "Honestly, I hardly ever see them anymore, I'm always so busy with Ashlee, Maree, and Courtnee." I tried not to groan, remembering how Lila had convinced all of her new friends to spell their names with *ee* endings. I mean, gag mee.

Of course, I would have gladly hung with the Double E's if it meant getting out of SVJH and hanging with Lila again. I wondered whether Lila had missed me at all. She must—a little. Could hanging with the Double E's really be that great?

"Listen," I said to Lila, "I may be at a different school, but I didn't move away. You should call me when you guys are getting together. I still love a good party."

Lila smiled. "Well, I'm having a little get-together tonight at my house. Just girls. But I think it'll be fun. Think you can come? We have *so* much to catch up on!"

I stopped myself from jumping up and down and squealing. "Let me call you," I said casually as we got to my corner. "I have some plans. But I'll try to drop by if I can." I didn't really have any plans, and if I could manage to get out of the house after dinner, I was definitely going to Lila's. But I didn't want to look too eager. After all, I do have some pride.

"Great. I can't wait for us to hang out." Lila gave me a little hug, and I turned the corner and headed down to my house.

I watched her go for a minute. What an awesome day I'd had. How could I have forgotten about my old friends? Why hadn't I been hanging with them? I shook my head. Well, between my old friends and my new ones, things were definitely looking up.

I turned up the walk, wondering what Elizabeth would make for dinner. Mom and Dad were in Vancouver at some lawyer convention for Dad's job, so my twin, my brother, and I were taking turns with the cooking and cleaning. Tonight was Elizabeth's night.

Being "looked after" by our older brother, Steven, was such a joke. Steven can't even remember to put the cap back on the toothpaste, much less care for other human beings. The only good thing is that he isn't as strict as Mom and Dad. He lets us stay up late and blast the stereo. . . .

Jessica

At that moment I was struck with such a brilliant idea that I actually stopped in my tracks.

Mom and Dad were going to be gone until next Monday. That meant that the living room would be a parent-free zone on Saturday night. And Steven didn't really care what we did.

This was the perfect opportunity for a Saturday night slumber party!

I'd invite Lila and all of my other Sweet Valley Middle friends. Maybe I would invite a couple of SVJHers too, like Kristin and Bethel.

It was time to have some fun for a change.

Now all I had to do was get Steven to agree.

Family Album

Here's the first Halloween
You and I went trick or treating by ourselves.

I was a fairy princess.
You were a brave knight.

You must have taken this photo
Because you aren't in the picture.

Has anything changed since then?
Many years later, still,

I can't see you,
But I know you're there.

A n n a

I can't show it to them, I thought. *What if they think it's horrible? I'll die.*

My two best friends, Salvador del Valle and Elizabeth Wakefield, sat across from me at Sal's dining-room table. We were looking over possible layouts for the first issue of a school magazine the three of us were starting. My hands were shaking, so I sat on them. I didn't want Salvador and Elizabeth to know how nervous I was. If they knew I was scared, then they might pretend to like my poem out of sympathy or something. They were good friends—that was the problem. I didn't want them to put it in the 'zine if it stank.

Elizabeth shook her head. "We've only got three articles—my school-bus article, Salvador's uniform thing, and that fake lunch menu I wrote." She sighed. "We'll need more before we have a full first issue of the 'zine."

Now's the time to show them the poem. I opened

my mouth, but all that came out was a small choking noise.

"Are you okay?" Salvador asked. He whacked me on the back. Just call him Mr. Helpful.

"Thanks," I choked out. Elizabeth passed me the bottle of water she had been sipping from. I took a swallow. Then I inhaled a deep, cleansing breath.

"I—I have—well, I wrote this thing." I fumbled around in my binder and finally pulled out the poem. "It, you know, I think it needs some work, but maybe—"

Salvador snatched the paper out of my hands. "'Family Album,'" he read out loud. Elizabeth leaned in so she could read the poem over his shoulder.

The room was silent as they read. My body went cold from head to foot.

When he was finished, Salvador looked up at me. Our eyes locked, and for a minute I was afraid that I would start crying. Elizabeth read the poem over again. The silence stretched on. . . .

They aren't saying anything, I thought. *They hate it.*

"I love it," Elizabeth said softly. Salvador reached out and squeezed my hand. "I think this would look great on the front page," Elizabeth went on.

"You do?" I whispered. I blinked several times.

12

"Absolutely," Elizabeth said. Salvador nodded.

Are they just saying this because they feel sorry for me? I wondered. Salvador looked sympathetic, even a little sad. But Elizabeth looked . . . excited. "We could put a cool border around it so that it really pops off the page," she said. "Do you have any more poems, Anna?"

Any more poems? Sure—I had at least a *hundred* others just like this one. I had notebooks full of poems about my dead brother. But we didn't want a magazine full of depressing poetry, did we?

"Uh—I'm not sure I have anything else that would be right for the 'zine," I hedged.

"Submit everything you've got," Elizabeth said. "We'll look them over and publish whatever we can."

Submit everything? Every single poem about Tim? Had she gone nuts? It was one thing to include a single poem as sort of a tribute, but I didn't really want to share every single poem with the entire student body. They were just too painful. I looked over at Salvador, whose mouth was opening and closing without making any sound, like a fish. It was obvious that he was just as shocked at Elizabeth's reaction as I was and didn't know how to tell her what a bad, insensitive suggestion she'd just made. *It's so out of character for her to ignore someone's feelings like that,* I thought. That's when I realized: Elizabeth still didn't know about Tim.

Elizabeth had no idea what my poem was really about. She just liked it.

Why hadn't I ever told Elizabeth that my brother was killed by a drunk driver? I was just used to everyone knowing already, I guess. But Elizabeth and her twin sister, Jessica, were new to Sweet Valley Junior High this year. Naturally, they didn't know anything about anyone over here.

Salvador knew who the poem was about, of course. He's been my best friend since kindergarten, and sometimes I wondered if he knows more about me than I do.

I was still staring at him. I guess Sal had the same realization about Elizabeth that I'd had because he snapped his mouth shut. He glanced at me and gave an encouraging smile. "Well, Anna. How does it feel to be headed for the front page?" he asked. He leaned toward me, looking into my eyes. The chill I had felt earlier was replaced by a warm glow.

"I think it's great," I said quietly. "Just *great,*" I added, a little louder, so they would know how happy I was. "Do you really think it's good enough for page one?"

"I'm positive." Elizabeth reached for the dummy

pages she had been roughing out and started talking about column inches, inserts, banners, etc.

I wasn't even listening. *Page one,* I thought dizzily. *Page one!*

Elizabeth had been the head of a newspaper at her old school, so she knew all of the details that went into putting this kind of thing together. Without Elizabeth, Salvador and I wouldn't have had a clue. Plus she was super-organized—not my strength, and *definitely* not Salvador's.

Elizabeth marked something down on a piece of paper. "Okay. Here's another thing," she said. "And it's pretty major. Does anyone have an idea for the name of the 'zine?"

"Why don't we call it *Salvador!*—you know, with an exclamation mark," Salvador said, holding up his hands like he was spelling his name out in lights. "That way people will know it's really cool."

"Next," Elizabeth said.

I laughed. "How about *Zone?*" I suggested.

"I like that!" Elizabeth said.

Salvador nodded. "Me too. Although it's not as good as *Salvador!*"

"*Zone* it is." Elizabeth looked at us. "This is getting too easy."

I grinned. "Well. I guess we're an awesome threesome."

Elizabeth tapped her pencil on her notebook. "We *are* a good team," she said. "But we should probably ask a few more people to join us. We can't do every 'zine all by ourselves. And we should start coming up with some policy ideas."

"What do you mean?" I asked. I didn't like the sound of the phrase "policy ideas." It's not like we were running *The Wall Street Journal* or something.

Elizabeth tightened her ponytail like she always does when she's ready to get down to business. "So far, you guys have let me make most of the decisions. But the whole point of having our own 'zine was to give everybody more freedom and more power."

Salvador looked as confused as I felt. "So what should we do? Hold elections or something?"

"No," she answered. "I just mean, how are we going to decide what to put in our 'zine? What if one of us likes something and the other two don't? Or vice versa?"

Salvador shrugged. "I don't know. So far, we've all agreed on everything."

"But we might not always agree," Elizabeth said.

Conflict resolution isn't my best sport. I pulled up the neck of my T-shirt and chewed on it. I do that when I get nervous. It's pretty gross, I know, but I can't help it.

Salvador looked at me and then at Elizabeth. "What do you think we should do?"

Elizabeth tapped her pencil on the table. "When I was in sixth grade, my friend Amy and I were the publishers of the paper. We decided that all decisions about what to run had to be unanimous."

Salvador leaned back in his seat. "So that means if one of us doesn't like something, we can veto it. Even if the other two like it?"

Elizabeth nodded.

"Okay by me," I said.

Salvador looked torn for a moment. Then he gave a quick nod. "Then *I* am no longer officially in charge," Elizabeth said. "We're *all* in charge."

"Except that you're the only one who knows anything about laying out a dummy and getting it printed," Salvador pointed out.

"I'll show you guys how to do it. It's easy," she said with a smile. "I'm glad that's all settled." She looked over the papers spread out in front of her. "Things are looking up now that we have Anna's poem."

I peered at the dummy. "How much more do we need before we can publish?" I asked.

Elizabeth poked at her blond ponytail with a pencil, thinking. "I'm not sure; it depends on the layout. I think we need at *least* one more piece—and it should be something different. Graphics, maybe?" She looked at Salvador. "How about a cartoon?"

Salvador reared back, but his black eyes sparkled. "Where in the world are we going to get a cartoon?" His voice was innocent, but he had turned bright red.

Elizabeth pointed her pencil at him. "I think we should have a Salvador del Valle original."

Salvador smiled and looked at me, but he was still blushing. Then he shrugged. "Actually, maybe I already have something here in my magic bag." He leaned over and pulled a folder out of his backpack.

Now I understood the red face. I felt the same way before I showed them my poem. Proud, ashamed, embarrassed, and scared all at the same time.

It's amazing how people just blush instead of spontaneously combusting as a result of all that internal pressure.

Salvador opened his folder and took out some sheets of drawing paper. I smiled at him, thinking about how supportive he had been when I showed my poem. I was going to do the same for him.

Elizabeth and I walked over to take a look.

After the first panel I could feel the smile freeze on my face.

Salvador's cartoon was about a superhero. She saves SVJH from the evil "Brainiacs" who threaten to force the students to think alike by poisoning the food in the cafeteria. But Wonder Girl outwits them by putting up posters for "brown bag lunch day."

It was kind of like how we had quit the obnoxious *Spectator* to start our own 'zine and rescue SVJH from dying of boredom.

Only—who was the heroine?

Was it a small Korean girl with a cynical attitude? Nope. The supergirl was blond. And perky.

And—here's another little clue—her secret identity is *Elspeth Warren*.

Duh!!!!!!!!!!!!!!!!!!!!

It was about *Elizabeth!*

I started feeling queasy, and the warm feelings I'd been having toward Salvador heated up to something more like rage.

Wonder Girl. *Wonder Girl?* I mean, spare me! Why didn't he just build a *shrine* to her?

Elizabeth's lips were curved in this pleased smile. And when her eyes got to the end of the strip, she began to applaud. "This is fantastic. It's *so* funny. Where did you get this idea, Salvador?"

Salvador looked like he might die of embarrassment. I could tell he was trying to read Elizabeth's expression. So was I. Did she know it was about her or not? "Well," Salvador said, "the muse works in mysterious ways."

I did not gag, amazingly.

19

"With this cartoon, I think we've got enough content to put out an issue," Elizabeth said. "Anna?"

I stared hard at Elizabeth. She was giving me this bright-eyed, innocent look.

Was it possible that Elizabeth really hadn't clued in? Or was she just pretending not to get it because she didn't know how to deal with Salvador's crush on her?

How could she not *know?* I mean, the character was called Elspeth Warren! Why didn't Salvador just name her Elizabetha Wakefielda and stop insulting everyone's intelligence?

I was furious at both of them. "I think it's still a little rough," I said.

Elizabeth's mouth fell open a bit. "What?"

Salvador bit his lip nervously. Like he knew exactly what I was thinking—but since he didn't know what *Elizabeth* was thinking, he wasn't going to say anything.

"I think it's a little rough," I repeated. "There's a lot riding on this first issue. We can't afford to look amateurish."

"But . . . ," Elizabeth began.

"Were you serious about us all agreeing or not?" I snapped.

Elizabeth tugged her earlobe. "Yes. Of course. I guess I just thought it was a good strip."

"I think it's a good strip too," I said. Then I

looked Salvador right in the eye. "But I think we need to be better than that for the first issue. Why don't you work on it a little more, Salvador?" He looked like I had punched him in the stomach, but I didn't care. Had he thought about how I might feel, having this strip thrown in my face? Did it ever occur to him that it might bother me that he liked Elizabeth better than he liked me?

Salvador's blush faded, and instead of angry and embarrassed, he looked ashamed. "She's right," he said, quickly taking up the sheets and putting them back in the folder. "It's too rough. I'll work on it some more and bring it back." Salvador grinned wryly.

"Okay," Elizabeth said, and sighed. "So I guess that's it, then." She checked her watch. "Just in time to go home and make dinner. It's already five."

"It *is*?" I jumped up, my heart beating quickly. "Ohmigosh. I have to get going—I told my mom I'd be back early. The plumber is coming to fix the kitchen sink, and—" I broke off. I'd been about to say, *"and you know how Mom is."*

But Elizabeth didn't really know about my mom, just like she didn't know about Tim. And even though Elizabeth was a friend now, I wasn't ready to talk to her about the home thing. About how my mom wasn't exactly operating at her

Anna

peak. How sometimes she wasn't exactly operating at all—which is why I had to call the plumber and then be home to let him in.

My mom sleeps a lot, even during the day. If I weren't home to let the plumber in, she might never even hear the doorbell.

Mom is kind of hard to explain to someone, though. I like Elizabeth a lot, and I don't want her to think my mom is a bad person or something—she's just kind of . . . sad.

I don't know why I think Elizabeth wouldn't understand. It's just that she seems to have this perfect family. (Unless you count her cooler-than-thou twin, Jessica.) Perfect mom. Perfect dad. Perfect brother. Perfect house. All of this perfection goes perfectly with Elizabeth's perfect California-blond good looks and straight-A perfect brain. Not that I'm jealous or anything.

I could really hate a person like that, but Elizabeth is so nice that it's hard to hold a grudge.

Hard, but not impossible.

Salvador

"You never make a blunder, Wonder Girl!" I sang as I walked down the street. I'd just had dinner with my grandmother—the Doña—and I was headed toward Anna's house. I go over there practically every night after dinner, but this time I was on a mission—to see if Anna had any suggestions for my comic strip. Of course, from the way she'd acted at the *Zone* meeting, I had a feeling Anna's only suggestion might be to set *Wonder Girl* over an open flame.

Still, I had to try.

I just wish I had realized Wonder Girl's true identity before the meeting. And by "true identity," I don't mean Elspeth Warren. I mean *Elizabeth.* The fact is, I hadn't even realized how much Elspeth was like Elizabeth until I saw it written all over Anna's face. Of course, it kind of made sense that I would wind up writing a comic about Elizabeth. I have her on the brain practically 24/7.

But what could I do? I mean, the only reason I wrote the strip in the first place was to try to think about something *other* than Elizabeth. That's how pathetic I am.

I have this letter up in my room. It's a letter to Elizabeth. In it I tell her how incredibly pretty and sweet and smart she is. I'd never mail it to her, of course. It's way too corny. The problem is, it's really easy to fall for Elizabeth—I'm sure half the guys at school think she's as beautiful as I do. I'm always worried that some other guy will get a crush on her for those reasons and she'll decide she likes him. But I know, *I know* that nobody can ever feel about Elizabeth the way I do. I see things that nobody else sees. I see the way she treats every single person she talks to with respect. I see the fact that she really, truly cares about people— like me, for example, and Anna. And I see that she's responsible—I would trust her with my life. Come to think of it, I would trust her with my life even more than I trust myself—she's *that* responsible. Elizabeth is the most incredible person I have ever met. And even though I know she doesn't feel the same way about me, I don't even care. I believe that one day, she will realize that I am the only person who really sees everything there is to see about her.

And that's when she and I will be together.

But first I had to start fixing the comic strip. After all, I didn't want Elizabeth to think that I was some loser who couldn't even write anything good enough to go in the 'zine I helped start.

I pictured Elizabeth's face when she read *Wonder Girl.* Had she seen the resemblance between Elspeth and herself? I couldn't tell. I *hoped* not.

One day I would tell Elizabeth how I felt about her. But I wouldn't do it through a comic strip. The time had to be right.

I was so focused on my thoughts about Elizabeth that I actually walked right by Anna's house. I looked up, and I was at the end of her block; I had to backtrack.

Someday I will no longer be a total spaz, I thought as I trudged back up the street. *Just not today.*

I rang the doorbell. *Wouldn't it be great if Anna had some brilliant suggestions for the strip?* I thought. *Then I could redo it so that it was hilarious and wonderful, and Elizabeth would read it and think that I was hilarious and wonderful. "Oh, Salvador,"* she would say, *"you're such a comic genius!" Then she would throw her arms around me and . . .*

Anna's door flew open. "Let's get out of here," she said, rushing past me, across the porch and down the front steps. She didn't look back.

"Anna!" I called. I reached over and shut the door, then followed her. "Wait!"

25

She wheeled around to face me. Her face was blotchy, and her eyes were red. Her hair was messy too, which was unusual for Anna.

I knew what all of this meant. Her mother was having a Bad Day.

"Oh, Anna," I said. I slipped my arms around her. That's when she really started crying. It was one of those cries where your whole body gets into it and you can't breathe. I didn't know what to say, so I just said, "It's okay, it's okay," over and over and kept on hugging her. It was stupid, I know, because it was so obviously *not* okay, but what else could I do?

Finally she seemed to calm down a little bit, and I loosened my iron grip on her. I kind of patted her hair awkwardly, and she took a few deep breaths and then sniffled a little.

"I th-think," she said, and sniffled again, "that I g-got some snot on you." She looked up at me, and her chin quivered a bit. "I'm s-sorry."

"It's okay," I told her. "I've always hated this shirt."

Anna laughed and wiped her face with her hands.

At that moment I would have given a million bucks to be the kind of guy who carries around a handkerchief.

I put my arm around her shoulders, and we headed down the street slowly. We didn't say anything for a couple of blocks. I racked my brain the entire way, trying to think of something sensitive and funny to say that would make her feel better, but I drew a blank. A dull ache settled over my heart. Tim had been my friend too. I still missed him. But I knew that it had to be about a thousand times worse for Anna. His absence was something she and her family lived with every day.

I looked at Anna out of the corner of my eye and saw her take a deep, shuddering breath. Then she shook her head, like she was trying to clear it.

"So," I said, "do you want to talk about it?"

"No," Anna said.

I nodded. You can't push these things. "Okay."

Then I guess she changed her mind because she said, "It was just . . ." She swallowed hard. "The *plumber*," she said in a tiny voice.

This caught me totally off guard. "*What?*"

The look on my face must have been pretty hilarious because Anna gave a little hiccup-giggle and repeated, "The plumber." She took a deep breath, and the tears started flowing again. Silently, though. "He said that he has to replace all of the bathroom pipes and that it's going to cost a lot of money. . . ." A tear streaked its way down the side of her nose. "It's just"—Anna went on in an almost whisper—"I just couldn't tell if he was telling the *truth*. If he really needs to replace the pipes or if he just sees that I'm a kid and is trying to rip me off. And Mom was asleep, and Dad is always home late these days—I tried to call him, but he was in a meeting—and I didn't know what to *do,* you know?" Anna looked at me, and her face twisted up and turned red again. "So I sent him away, but in the meantime we can't use the *bathroom.*" She sniffed and wiped her nose.

"When Dad got home, he was *furious* that I hadn't just had the plumber fix everything. But how was I supposed to know? Why do *I* have to take care of everything?" She looked at the ground and shook her head slowly. "Everything's been kind of falling apart in the past few days. I mean, I'm sure you could tell that things have been worse than usual lately." Anna looked up at me again and smiled wryly. "That *I've* been worse than usual."

I nodded, even though it was a total lie. I felt hollow. I'd had no clue Anna was having a rough time. Well, no worse than normal, that is. *I am a horrible friend,* I thought. *What kind of person spends all of his time thinking about Elizabeth Wakefield when his best friend really needs him?* Suddenly I realized just how little attention I'd been giving to Anna—to *everything* that wasn't Elizabeth.

I reached out and gave Anna another hug. I'm not usually very touchy-feely, but I really didn't know what else I could do. Anna's arms went around my waist in a stranglehold. I felt afraid suddenly. I can't explain it. All I know is that I wanted to stay there and protect her.

"Oh, Salvador," she said, her words muffled into my shirt, "thanks."

I didn't say anything. I just squeezed her tighter and silently vowed to pay more attention to my best friend.

Anna and I had been friends forever, and I wanted to be sure to look out for her. To safeguard her.

To care for her like the brother she didn't have anymore.

Jessica

"And I thought that Salvador's comic was really funny, but Anna didn't seem to like it, so she rejected it, which I thought was kind of unfair, so—" Elizabeth had been babbling about the 'zine since before dinner, and she wasn't showing any signs of slowing down now that we were clearing the table. Steven had bolted upstairs after dinner, leaving me alone to hear the fascinating details of magazine life. Like I cared about the dumb 'zine. I couldn't believe that she actually found this stuff interesting. Why couldn't my twin be interested in something *normal*? Boys, for example. Or *parties*.

"I tried to let Salvador know that I thought it was good, but he still looked kind of hurt, and I felt really bad," Elizabeth went on. I had to change the subject—fast.

"So," I interrupted, "what's the deal with you two anyway?"

Elizabeth played dumb. "With me and Anna?"

31

"No." I rolled my eyes. "With you and *Salvador.*"

"There's no deal," Elizabeth said, suddenly concentrating intently on the dish she was holding.

I lifted my eyebrows. "Oh, *really?* Personally, I think he's got a major crush on you."

"He does not!" Elizabeth insisted. But then her cheeks turned pink. *Interesting. Does this crush go two ways?* I wondered. But before I could say anything, Elizabeth had escaped to the kitchen. "I've got to wash the dishes," she called over her shoulder, like she could get away that easily.

"I'll help," I offered, following her.

Elizabeth stopped, turned, and gave me a "who-are-you-and-what-have-you-done-with-my-sister?" look. "You'll *help?*" she repeated—like she couldn't believe her ears. "Okay, now I know you want something."

I nodded. "I want you to help me convince Steven to let me have a sleep over Saturday night." I turned on the water in the kitchen sink to show how truly helpful I was.

"He's not going to listen to *me,*" Elizabeth said. "Besides, I think he wants to have Cathy over on Saturday."

"I thought they broke up."

"They did," Elizabeth said. "But they're back together now."

Just what I needed—Steven smooching his

girlfriend on the couch in front of my friends. Why couldn't my brother just stay broken up with his girlfriend like a normal human being? "He could *go out* with Cathy," I suggested. "Then having a few friends over would be no problem."

"Gosh," Elizabeth said, opening her eyes really wide. "I can't imagine why anyone would have a problem with that idea. Except that Mom and Dad told Steven not to leave us by ourselves at night on penalty of death. And the last things they said before they pulled out of the driveway were 'don't make a mess' and 'absolutely no parties.'"

"Don't be cute," I said, annoyed. Of course, Elizabeth was right, but I wasn't ready to give up. This party concept was too good to abandon.

I squirted some detergent into the water and plunged the big spaghetti pot in, thinking hard. "Where are all the other dishes?" I asked as I scrubbed. I looked around the kitchen. She had already loaded the dishwasher—had she thrown everything else out the window? "There's hardly anything to clean up except this one pot. You'd hardly know anybody had been in here cooking."

"I cleaned up as I worked," Elizabeth said, and shrugged.

"That's it," I said.

"That's it?" Elizabeth asked. "You aren't going to rinse the pot?"

33

I rolled my eyes. I swear, sometimes I wonder about my twin. "No, that's it, I have the solution to our problem. You just said it—*clean up.* Mom and Dad never even have to know I had a party. We'll just clean up everything really well."

"The only problem with that," Elizabeth said, "is that it would be *you* and *your friends* cleaning up. Not me. Have you taken a good, long look at your room lately?"

Okay, did she *have* to bring up my messy room? But what did that have to do with anything? "Come on, Elizabeth," I begged. "Help me sweet-talk Steven into it." I passed her a plate, and she rinsed.

The phone rang. I wondered if it was for me—not that I got tons of calls lately, but still, it was possible. Oh, well. My hands were soapy. Steven would answer it.

"I don't know," Elizabeth said. "I'll think about it."

The phone rang again. What was taking him so long?

"We'll just wear Steven down with kindness until there's no way he can say no," I said.

The phone rang again.

"*Steven!*" I yelled. "*Get the phone, you moron, we're doing the dishes!*"

Elizabeth laughed. "If that's your idea of sweet-talking Steven, something tells me the party on Saturday night is a no go."

"*Jessica!* It's for you!" Steven yelled from the living room.

I wiped off my hands and grabbed the kitchen phone. I could hear music playing in the background. "Hello?"

"Hi. It's Lila. Just calling to see what your estimated time of arrival might be. Everyone is asking about you."

I couldn't help a little sigh. At dinner Steven had stubbornly refused to let me go out "on a school night." I hadn't heard from Lila in weeks. Why did Steven have to pick tonight to develop a shred of responsibility? Anyway, that was why I hadn't mentioned my little party idea to him yet.

"Oh, Lila, I'm so sorry. I can't make it." I didn't want Lila to think I was lame or anything, so I added a little improvisation. "I didn't realize it was so late. I had company for dinner and *he* just left."

Elizabeth stared at me.

"Oh?" Lila said, in her tell-me-more voice. "Anyone special?"

"*Very* special," I confirmed, winking at Elizabeth. She shook her head and went back to rinsing and drying the dishes.

"I can't believe you aren't coming!" Lila sounded really disappointed, which only made me want to go over there more. But I knew my party would never happen if Steven caught me sneaking out tonight. "When are we going to get to see you?" Lila asked.

"Well . . . ," I hedged. "I was thinking of having a get-together of my own this weekend."

Elizabeth whirled to face me, her eyes wide. "No!" she whispered.

I turned my back on her. "Saturday night," I went on. "The folks are away, so I thought it might be a good time for us to hang. But I'll have to let you know."

Lila giggled breathlessly. "Sounds cool! *Definitely* call me."

"Okay, then. G'night." I hung up the phone.

I turned and saw Elizabeth standing with her hands on her hips. "Don't go there," she warned.

"All I said was—"

"All you *said* was that you were going to have a party on Saturday night. Steven said no. Mom and Dad said no. And now *I'm* saying no."

Why did my twin have to be so lame? "What if Steven says yes?" I challenged.

She looked at me like I had just suggested Steven might sprout wings and fly. "He *won't*."

"But what if he did. Then what?"

Elizabeth pressed her lips together. Then she grinned. "Then I'd want to invite some of *my* friends over too."

A n n a

The sky was getting lighter and lighter—turning peach, then pink—as I sat on my front porch, waiting for Salvador to come by so we could walk to school together. It was going to be a beautiful day.

It was one of those mornings when everything seems extra clear. My granola had seemed sweeter, my milk creamier, my toothpaste mintier, my hair darker, my smile brighter. Everything was better than usual. That's what a good friend can do for you.

I had woken up thinking about Salvador. He had been so sweet to me the night before—so understanding—that I couldn't wait to see him today. You would have thought I had a crush on him or something, the way I was smiling as I brushed my hair.

"Hey, Anna!" Salvador called as he hurried up the walk to my house.

"Hi!" I said, feeling warm all over. Salvador's

Anna

hair was all disheveled, and his khakis were totally wrinkled. He'd probably just rolled out of
bed, as usual. Salvador has a tough time waking
up most days. He looked really cute.

He took the three steps up to my front porch
in one stride and bounded over to where I sat
on the swing. He bowed low and, with a flour-
ish, held out a black-eyed Susan.

I smiled. "For me?"

"Of course," Salvador said as he straightened
up. "Freshly picked. Of course, I'll deny it if
Mrs. Petersen next door ever mentions it."

I giggled and took the flower. "How do I
look?" I asked as I tucked it behind my ear.

"Like a vision of loveliness." He clutched his
heart.

I rolled my eyes and stood up.

"Like the sun rising in its glory," Salvador
went on in a phony accent. "Like the immortal
goddess Aphrodite—"

I laughed and socked him on the shoulder.
"Time for school, Romeo."

He grinned. "Let's go."

I was so happy as we walked to school that I
actually felt like humming. I reined it in,
though. I didn't want to seem crazy. *I can't believe Salvador brought me flowers*, I thought. *Well,
flower. But still.* That was so, well . . . I couldn't

38

think of any other word besides *romantic*.

About five blocks from school Salvador started fiddling with his hair. Suddenly he turned to me. "Does my hair look dumb?" he asked.

"No worse than usual," I said.

He frowned. "Thanks a lot."

"I'm just *kidding,* Salvador. You look fine. *Great,*" I amended when he didn't seem satisfied with *fine.* "What's up with you?" I asked.

"Oh," he said. "Nothing."

"Come on, Salvador. You were just happy a minute ago," I said gently. Salvador had been so sweet to me the night before, I was eager for my chance to help him now. "Is something up at school?" I prodded. "Are you freaking about some test that I've forgotten about?"

"No, it's not that. I just—" He looked pained. "Anna, what do you do when—you have feelings for someone and—they just think you're friends?"

My heart stopped. I'm not kidding; it actually stopped beating. Then it started up again—at about five times the normal speed. What was he saying?

"I—I don't know," I said breathlessly. First the flower, now this . . . Was Salvador saying that he was *falling* for me? "I guess you have to tell the person how you feel," I said. Finally. Salvador smiled sadly.

"It's not that easy," he said.

I looked into his warm, black eyes. "I know." Suddenly my knees felt rubbery and my head felt like it was disconnected from my body. I was floating outside myself, watching this happen from a distance.

"I try not to think about it," Salvador went on. "But the harder I try, the more out of control it all gets." He looked at me and bit his lip. "I'm sorry, Anna," he said. "I know you probably don't want to hear about all of this."

His words echoed in my head. *I'm sorry, Anna. I'm sorry, Anna. I'm sorry, Anna.* I cleared my throat. "Don't worry about it," I told him. "These things happen."

"Well, whatever," he said, and started walking even more quickly. "I'm not going to solve this problem before school."

Slowly my heartbeat returned to normal. I gave silent thanks that Salvador hadn't actually come out and confessed anything to me before we got to SVJH. I don't know what I would have said.

And the reason for that, I realized with a jolt, *is because I'm no longer sure how I feel about Salvador.*

Jessica

". . . wash your car twice a week, make your bed every morning, and do your laundry once a month."

"Once a week," Steven corrected.

"Once a *month!*" I insisted, looking down at my notes.

"Once a week or the deal's off," Steven said.

I narrowed my eyes at him. We had been negotiating for almost half an hour, and I still had to finish getting ready for school. At first he'd said no deal, no way—in spite of the fact that I'd brought him breakfast in bed. But when I convinced him it would only be a few girls at my party and that he didn't have to do anything at all except stay out of the way, he agreed to at least discuss it.

I guess Steven could tell that I wasn't going to cave on this one because eventually he waved his arm at me. "That's it. Deal's off."

"All right!" I groaned. "Once a *week.*"

Jessica

Steven sat back down and smiled. "Okay. Deal's back on for Saturday night."

I breathed a sigh of relief. "I'll take care of everything," I assured him. "Shopping, cleaning, everything."

"I hope you realize I'm canceling a date with Cathy so you can have this party," Steven said, frowning. As if that was some big sacrifice. I've met Cathy, and, if you ask me, Steven should be thanking me that I'm letting him hang with my friends instead.

"You won't regret it." I ran upstairs and stuck my head in Elizabeth's room. She was already dressed and making her bed. "It's a go!" I said.

Elizabeth's jaw dropped. "You're *kidding*."

"No. All you have to do is wash Steven's car twice a week, make his bed every morning, and do his laundry once a week for the next three months."

She gave me a level look. "And then you woke up."

"I had to try," I said, grinning. I couldn't believe it—this party was actually going to happen! I couldn't wait to call Lila tonight and tell her. This was going to be so much fun. Jessica Wakefield was back—and better than ever!

I spent the entire bus ride to school planning my outfit and hair. Everything had to be perfect. I thought about decorations and music as I walked down the hall. I could hardly wait to start inviting people.

I saw Kristin standing by her locker. "Kristin!" I shouted. Kristin turned around and smiled. Then she glanced over at the person next to her, and a chill settled over my body. It was Lacey Frells, the coolest girl at SVJH. Lacey didn't like me much. She frowned as I walked over, and for a second I considered running in the opposite direction.

I have a right to talk to Kristin if I want to, I told myself. Kristin was Lacey's best friend even though they were totally different. Kristin is very popular, but she's also outgoing and friendly. Lacey has a mean streak a mile wide. A few weeks ago she had asked me to lie for her so that she could hang with her friends after school. Eventually I told her that I wouldn't do it. Lacey has been giving me evil glares ever since then. But Kristin didn't seem to be holding a grudge against me, even though I'm sure she'd heard the story. I guess she knew I did the right thing.

Basically, when I say that the cool crowd at SVJH has been kind of mean to me, I'm talking about Lacey.

I momentarily considered inviting Kristin to the party some other time. But then I changed my mind. Lacey was so used to ditching me for her "cooler" friends, why not give her a taste of her own medicine? Let's see how she liked feeling left out.

"Just wanted to invite you to a little party

Saturday night," I said, looking directly at Kristin.

Lacey sneered. "Is it a *thlumber* party?" she asked, lisping in a little girl's voice like a slumber party was the most babyish idea in the world.

I wanted to kill her, but I have to admit, I felt kind of lucky she said it. "Of course not," I said, rolling my eyes like the idea of a slumber party was just too ridiculous for words. "Just a party party. My parents are going to be out of town and . . ."

"Whoaaa!" Kristin laughed. "This is a chaperon-free party?"

"Not exactly," I said. "My brother, Steven, will be there," I added in a blasé voice.

Lacey's eyebrows shot up, but I couldn't read her expression. "You mean your *boyfriend?*"

I wanted to die right there. Why had I brought up my stupid brother? For a while I had pretended that Steven was my boyfriend because I figured Lacey would be impressed if she thought I was dating someone in high school. It had totally backfired.

I knew my face was red, but I managed to say, "He's my *brother.*"

Lacey waved her hand in a spare-me gesture and said, "Yeah, yeah. Gel knows who he is." *Any opportunity to drop in a reference to her high-school boyfriend,* I thought. Lacey tapped her finger against her cheek. "That could be fun. What time?"

What? I hadn't even invited her! I felt my mouth drop open, but I couldn't think of anything to say. "Uh—uh—"

Lacey looked annoyed. I couldn't blame her. I must have looked like a freak, standing there and stammering. I had to face it—I was trapped. I couldn't tell Lacey that she wasn't invited without looking really rude in front of Kristin. Oh, well. Maybe if Lacey had a good time at the party, she would stop giving me icy stares all the time.

"What time is the party?" Lacey repeated slowly, as if she were talking to an idiot.

"Sevenish," I answered finally, trying to sound sophisticated and breezy.

"Great," Kristin said. "Can I bring anything?"

"No thanks," I told her. "I'll take care of everything."

"Who else is going to be there?" Lacey asked.

"My old friends from Sweet Valley Middle."

Kristin gave a wide smile. "We're psyched. Right, Lace?"

Lacey hesitated. "Hmmm," she said. I wondered whether that meant something more like "yes" or more like "we'll see." Lacey gave me a tight smile and walked away.

"Don't mind Lacey," Kristin said. "She's still a little mad at you, but she'll get over it by Saturday night."

"I *hope* so," I said. But now I had a new problem.

If Lacey was coming to the party, I wasn't sure if I should still invite Bethel. Those two did *not* get along. Bethel was the one who convinced me to stand up to Lacey—and Lacey knew it. I figured Kristin would know what was best. "Think it's okay to ask Bethel?"

Kristin shrugged. "Like I said, Lacey will probably be over it by Saturday. I wouldn't worry about it."

I felt better. I didn't want to risk offending Bethel by not inviting her. But the truth was, if it was going to make for a majorly bad scene with Lacey, then I would have blown Bethel off. I didn't want my old friends to have to deal with a scene like that.

"Okay," I told Kristin. "Thanks."

"See you," Kristin said, closing her locker.

I hurried on down the hall, keeping an eye out for Bethel.

I spotted her looking at something on the bulletin board at the end of the hall and walked over to her.

"Hi, Bethel!"

"Hey, Jessica. You ready to break some records next week?" She grinned.

"Always," I replied. "You ready to party on Saturday?"

Bethel lifted her eyebrows. "Whose party is it?"

"Mine. I'm having some friends over on Saturday night. Can you come?"

"Sure—sounds great. Should I bring some cookies or something?"

What was the deal with everyone offering to bring something? My old crew never offered to bring anything—or clean anything up either. "Just bring yourself."

The bell rang. "Okay. If you change your mind, let me know." Bethel strode off down the hall. I was glad I had invited her.

I made a quick stop at my locker (thankfully, my locker partner, Ronald Rheece, aka King Doofus, wasn't there) and then headed for class. I couldn't wait for school to be over. I wanted to get home, call Lila, and get the ball rolling.

By the time I got home, I had the whole party mapped out: food, music, dancing—it was going to be a blast. Luckily Steven wasn't home, so I could have a little privacy.

I went into the kitchen, got myself a soda, and picked up the phone. Before I punched in Lila's number, I took some deep breaths so I wouldn't sound too eager or excited.

"Helleeeeeeew?" Lila's voice sounded deeper than usual, and she drew out the word so that it had about five syllables.

I snorted. "What's with the vamp voice?"

There was a long pause while Lila tried to decide whether or not to pretend she didn't know what I was talking about. She must have decided there wasn't much point in putting me on because she laughed. "I was hoping you were a guy."

"Any guy? Or one guy in particular?" I took a sip of my soda.

"One guy in particular," Lila answered. "He calls a lot, actually."

"What's his name?"

"Roary Michaels."

I'd heard that name. From Steven. Roary Michaels was in high school!

"I hope you don't mind," Lila went on to say, "but I invited Roary to your party Saturday night."

I stared at the phone. *Lila* invited *Roary* to *my* party? Had she gone *insane?* First of all, I hadn't even told her for sure that I was *having* a party. Second, where did she get off inviting guys to my party? Third, how did she know it wasn't a slumber party? And fourth . . .

"In fact, I've invited a bunch of people. The old crowd is coming, and so are Ashlee, Maree, and Courtnee. Plus I told Roary to bring some of his friends."

Roary's friends! Roary's friends as in . . . high-school guys? What was Steven going to say? I'd told him it was just girls!

"Jessica? Are you there?"

"I'm here," I said quickly.

"It's okay that I invited them, isn't it?"

"Oh, sure," I said. My whole body had gone numb. I don't know why I felt like it would be impossible to tell Lila not to bring Roary and his friends. I just couldn't do it somehow. I didn't want her to think I'd gotten less cool than I used to be.

"I just thought that with no parents around, who's going to mind?" Lila explained. "Not Steven. I mean, some of these guys are his friends too."

"Oh, absolutely," I agreed, my mind racing. Lila was right. How could Steven get mad about guys coming over when the guys were friends of his?

"Besides," she went on, "some of them are really *cute*. You should be thanking me, Jessica."

I giggled. Cute guys—now that was an argument I understood. Wow. This party was going to be even cooler than I thought!

The question was: (*a*) Tell Steven now? (*b*) Tell him later? Or (*c*) Don't tell him at all and let him be pleasantly surprised by the appearance of his friends the night of the party?

Just then Steven came banging through the back door of the kitchen, scowling. "Hope you enjoy your little party on Saturday night," he snarled. "Because Cathy is really mad at me for breaking our date."

Well, for sure the answer wasn't *a*.

Elizabeth

If I was going to invite some of my old friends to our slumber party, I had to get rolling—after all, the party was in two days! There were so many people I hadn't seen in forever, for a moment I couldn't decide who to invite first. Then it hit me—Maria Slater. She and I had been really close for years, and I hadn't talked to her in over a month! She picked up after the first ring.

"Hello?"

"Hello, Maria?" I said. "It's Elizabeth!"

I'd expected her to squeal or sound happy, but instead she just said, "Elizabeth?" and I realized that she didn't know who I was.

"Elizabeth *Wakefield*," I said, trying not to feel hurt.

"Oh, *hi!*" She sounded pleased. "I haven't heard from you in so long!" It was true, although she hadn't called me either. "How are you? How's the new school?"

"Oh, great," I said. "I love it. How about you?"

Elizabeth

"You know SVMS," Maria said. "Nothing ever changes."

I couldn't think of anything to say to that, and there was a semi-awkward pause. Weird. We used to talk for hours on end before I left Sweet Valley Middle. "So—I'm calling to invite you to a party this Saturday," I said finally. "I want you to meet some of my new friends." I was thinking of Anna, who I'd already called. She was definitely coming. I was kind of sad that I couldn't invite Salvador too. But he wouldn't exactly fit in at an all-girls slumber party.

"This Saturday?" Maria repeated. "Oh no! I can't."

"Oh," I said. I tried to keep the disappointment out of my voice. I hadn't seen her in forever, and now she was saying no to my party?

"I'm really sorry, Elizabeth. My family is going to New York this weekend. My sister, Nina, has an audition for some music program. She's been practicing for weeks—there's no way I can get out of it."

She'd known about this for weeks? And I was just finding out *now?* We really had been out of touch. . . . "Well, that should be fun, right? New York and all."

"Yeah. We're going to stay in a hotel, see Broadway shows, eat out, and make it a big party weekend so that Nina won't feel bad if she doesn't get into the school."

"That's great." I tried to sound like I meant it.

"I'm sorry I can't come," she said. She didn't really sound all that sorry, though.

"That's okay," I told her. "Next time."

"Next time," she echoed. But I had to wonder if there would ever be a next time. Somehow I doubted it.

Jessica stuck her head in the doorway just as I hung up the phone. She was holding a pad of paper.

"Who are you inviting?" she asked. "I'm making the guest list."

"Anna," I said.

She marked it down. "Who else?"

I hesitated. "That's it."

"That's *it?*" Jessica asked. She looked shocked. "Really?"

I nodded. "Yeah."

"Ooooh-kaaay," Jessica said, "that sure was easy." She went back to her room.

I sat on my bed, thinking. *I really should call some of my other old friends.* But I didn't want to. My conversation with Maria made me feel so strange, like I wasn't sure who my friends were all of a sudden.

I glanced over at the phone again, and it rang, making me jump. I picked it up.

"Maria?" I asked, thinking maybe she was calling to tell me that her trip had been canceled.

Elizabeth

"Elizabeth?" The voice on the other end sounded confused. "Is that you?"

"Mom!"

"Hi! How is everything? Has the house burned down?" she joked.

I laughed. "Not yet. Everything's under control." The slumber party popped into my brain, and I felt kind of bad about not mentioning it. *But I'm only inviting one person,* I reasoned. *It's not like this is going to be some wild party.* "How's the convention?"

"We're having a great time. Your dad is at a lecture right now—I think he's enjoying this even more than I am."

I suddenly felt sad. Just hearing my mom's voice made me miss my parents. A lot. "I wish you were here," I said.

"Oh, sweetheart, I miss you too," Mom said. Then she laughed. "I hope Steven isn't being too strict."

"You'll have to talk to Jessica about that."

"Actually, I would love to. Is she there?"

"Let me get her." I walked through the bathroom and into Jessica's room, where she was sitting on her bed, poring over the party list.

"Mom's on the phone," I told her.

Jessica squealed, jumped off the bed, and made a grab for the phone.

"Hold on," I said, yanking it out of her reach.

I held it up to my ear. "Here she is, Mom. I miss you."

"I miss you too, sweetie. I'll see you in a few days."

"Okay. I love you, Mom."

"Same here, honey. Good night."

"Bye." I handed the phone to my twin.

"Mom!" I heard Jessica shout as I headed back to my room, feeling even lonelier than before. I had to get my mind on something else.

I turned to my desk to get my homework started, and my eye fell on *Wonder Girl*. Today at school I'd asked Salvador if I could take another look at it. I had thought it was great at the meeting—but I was starting to doubt my judgment where Salvador was concerned. I mean, did I think *Wonder Girl* was great just because I thought everything Salvador did was great? It was possible. *Maybe I can figure out some ways to improve it,* I thought as I read it over. When I came to the last panel, I shook my head. *Anna is dead wrong,* I decided. *This is really funny.*

I picked up the comic, then got out the *Zone* dummy. I started rearranging the articles and Anna's poem. At first I couldn't make everything fit. But I moved Anna's poem to the middle so that it covered two pages and had a really neat border.

Elizabeth

Then I put *Wonder Girl* on the front. It looked great.

Maybe on Saturday, during the party, I'd have a chance to take Anna aside, show her how good *Wonder Girl* looked, and see if I could get her to change her mind.

I hoped so. Every time I pictured the look on Salvador's face when Anna criticized his strip, I got this little ache around my heart.

Jessica

It was Friday, and the atmosphere in the hall had that day-before-the-weekend feeling.

I was so excited about my party tomorrow night that I was humming a little tune as I spun the combination on my locker. Recently I had figured out that if I waited until just seven minutes before the first bell, I could avoid my locker partner, Ronald. He always had to rush to make his special bus for brainiac class, which just put that extra sheen on my day. No doubt about it, my future was looking bright—

"Jessica," said a voice behind me.

I knew even before I turned that it was Lacey. I took my time gathering my notebooks, then casually flipped my hair over my shoulder.

"Oh, hi, Lacey," I said. *You're not the only one who knows how to act cool,* I thought.

Lacey cocked an eyebrow. "Headed to class?"

"Sure," I replied. As we started walking down the hall together, I realized that one of the things that gave Lacey her major cool aura was that she never hurried. She sort of slunk from one classroom to the other. Well, two could play that game.

I pushed my hips forward a little and let my shoulders droop—like Lacey. "So, are you ready for the party?" Suddenly I was really happy that Lacey was coming. I was looking forward to dropping in the fact that there were going to be high-school guys there. *You're not the only one with connections, honey.*

Lacey shook her chestnut hair back out of her eyes. "Talk away," she invited.

"Little change of plans. There are going to be some guys, and—"

She snorted. "No kidding," she interrupted, "I already invited Gel."

I stopped in my tracks. "You invited Gel?" I repeated, unable to keep the surprise out of my voice.

Lacey looked slightly offended. "I thought you said it was a *party*. If you invited me, I assumed you meant Gel could come too. You wouldn't expect me to go out on a Saturday night without him, would you?"

"Oh no!" I said quickly, even though it was a big lie. I hadn't thought about Gel one way or the other. But if he wanted to come, I guessed it would be okay. He wasn't a friend of Steven's, but maybe he knew Roary and that crew. He could just kind of blend in with them.

"Gel will probably bring some of his friends," Lacey went on. "You know how guys are. They don't go anyplace if they think they won't know anybody."

My smile froze on my face, but I tried to act natural. *It's going to be fine,* I told myself. After all, how many people could Gel possibly bring?

"We don't have to come," Lacey said suddenly, like she was mad that I wasn't acting enthusiastic about Gel and his friends.

"No, no!" I protested. Don't ask me why I didn't just say, "Yeah, Lacey, I don't really want you or your dumb boyfriend at my party." I guess the truth was, I kind of *did* want them there. If Lacey was ready to be friends, well, then so was I. "I want you guys to come. Really."

"If it's going to be some kind of big problem . . ."

"It's not," I said quickly. Somehow I'd make sure it wasn't. Even if it meant locking Steven in the garage.

I thought Gel and his over-Depped hair were pretty gross, but that didn't mean other people thought so. He was cool, and I bet his friends were too.

"I have to talk to Kristin before first bell," Lacey said once we were just outside our classroom. "Later." She slouched away.

"See you, Lacey."

I stood there a moment, thinking. Things were working out even better than I dreamed. Without even trying, I was throwing the party of the millennium. By Monday morning nobody at Sweet Valley Junior High would ever say *"Jessica who?"* again. I was headed back where I belonged.

In fact, I felt very cool and popular already. I checked my watch—still a few minutes before first bell. I decided to fix my hair and lip gloss before class. If I was going to be popular, I had to look the part. I slunk down the hall toward the girls' room, shoulders drooping, hips swiveling forward. I let my hair fall forward so I was looking out the center of the curtain.

Visibility was limited. But the look was so good, it was worth the minor inconvenience of not being able to see anything.

I looked cool. I looked in control. I looked . . .

"Ouch!" somebody said.

. . . like a klutz. "Sorry," I said, pushing my hair back so I could see who I'd just plowed into.

"No problem." It was Brian Rainey, Elizabeth's very cute locker partner. He was giving me a smile—which was pretty nice, considering I'd just stepped right on his toe and pushed him into a bank of lockers.

"Are you all right? I didn't see you, and . . ."

"It's okay. It's okay. Don't worry about it." Brian walked around in a circle, testing his toe.

"Anything broken?"

"Nah!"

"Will you be able to run this afternoon?" Brian was on the boys' cross-country team.

"Oh, sure. Nothing's going to keep me out of competition."

I wondered if he was just saying that. But I didn't really care—I was just glad he was being so nice about it. I had a sudden brainstorm. Why should I let Lila and Lacey invite all of the guys? "I'd love to talk track sometime. Why don't you come over Saturday night? I'm having a little party."

His face lit up. "Cool. What kind of party?"

I tried to sound nonchalant. "Just some guys and some girls. We'll play a few CDs. Hang out. Maybe dance. My folks are out of town, so it seemed like a good weekend to do it."

Brian nodded. "Great. I'll be there. What time?"

"Seven."

"Seven it is. See you then." Brian gave me another grin and a wave, then hurried off.

I waved after him happily.

For the first time in a long time, I felt like everything made sense. Like I was myself again.

Gel,

You know that guy you don't like—Steven Wakefield? Well, guess what? His sister invited us to a party Saturday night, and Steven the Dork is the chaperon. What a laugh—I'm sure he wouldn't even notice if we totally trashed the place. I've been spreading the word. Things could get kind of wild. I hope.

Tell all your friends—it's time to party!

Lacey

Elizabeth

I had just gotten to school when Salvador walked up to me. He leaned against the locker next to mine. "Are you mad at me?" he asked.

"What?"

He gave me a nervous smile. "You mad at me or something? Listen, if it's about *Wonder Girl . . .*"

"I'm not mad at you," I told him. "Why would I be?" This conversation wasn't making much sense. "As a matter of fact, I dummied up the 'zine and I put *Wonder Girl* on the front page. I was going to show it to Anna tomorrow and see if I could get her to change her mind."

Salvador grinned. "Really? So you're not mad?"

"No. Why would you think that?"

"Because you didn't invite me to your party," he answered.

"It's all girls!"

He shook his head. "Not anymore. Everybody's talking about it. It sounds like the party of the semester."

I gasped. "Hold it. Where did you hear this?"

"At my locker. Then at the water fountain. Then in the boys' room. What's the matter? Why are you looking at me like that?"

"Because the last time I talked to Jessica about this party, it was a slumber party and it was all girls. Now it sounds like the whole school is going to be there."

Salvador nodded. "Maybe more than that."

I turned my locker dial. Suddenly I couldn't remember the combination.

"You didn't know?"

I shook my head. "No. And I doubt that Steven knows either. I swear, I am going to strangle Jessica! This is *so* typical."

Salvador gave me this crooked smile. He didn't say anything for a long moment.

"So, is there anything I can do?" he asked finally.

I shook my head. "No. There's nothing even I can do now. If the word's out that the party's on, then it's on."

"Uh—so can I come?"

I smiled. "Yes. Of course. You and Anna. Maybe I'll even invite more of my old friends." I chewed on a nail nervously. "Maria can't come, but maybe Todd could make it—"

"Who's that?" Salvador asked. He had a weird look on his face.

I felt a blush creep up my neck and over my face. "What? Oh, he's, well, he's just this guy I used to be—friends with. At Sweet Valley Middle." I smiled nervously. The fact was, Todd used to sort of be my boyfriend. We went to dances together, stuff like that. But for some reason, I really didn't want to say that to Salvador. "Good old Todd," I added. "What a good *friend.*" I knew I sounded like a total nerd, but somehow I couldn't stop talking. "Maybe he can help keep things under control."

Salvador just stood there a moment, looking at me. "*I'll* help you," he said. "And so will Anna."

I gave him a weak smile.

"Besides, I bet you won't even need any help," he added confidently. "You're Elizabeth the Wonder Girl. See you later."

As I watched him walk off, my heart rate slowly returned to normal. In a flash my locker combination came back to me. I opened my locker and sorted through my books mechanically, my mind racing. How was Steven going to react? Was he going to be mad at me too? And how many people were going to come?

I slammed my locker and headed down the hall. It wasn't until I was almost at my first-period class that Salvador's words sank in. "You're Elizabeth the Wonder Girl."

Elizabeth

Wait a minute. He just called me Wonder Girl.

Wait *a minute. Wonder Girl's name is Elspeth Warren.*

No—wait a minute—*Wonder Girl looks* exactly like me.

I couldn't believe it. How could I have been so *dumb?*

My face began to feel hot, and I could feel myself blushing beet red. My heart gave a big thump. My knees felt like they were made of lead.

I was so embarrassed, I actually groaned out loud.

I couldn't deal with my first-period class just then. I checked my watch. Four minutes. Good. I darted into the girls' room and splashed some water on my face, trying to pull my thoughts together.

What did Salvador think? Did he think I was too stupid to get it? What was there to get anyway? So he wrote a comic about me—what did *that* mean?

Was he—was he *making fun* of me? My eyes started to tear up, and my mind raced through the comic. *But Salvador isn't the kind of guy who would purposely try to hurt someone's feelings,* I told myself. *Besides, Wonder Girl is a* cool *character.* So, then, what else could it mean? My heart

66

thumped loudly. Was it possible that he—that Salvador *liked* me?

I turned on the water really hard so I could groan again and nobody would hear me.

At the beginning of school Salvador had asked me out on a date-ish thing. Unfortunately he had blown off some plans with Anna to do it, so when she found out, she was pretty mad at him. So was I, and I let him know it. I'd told him no more dates, and he'd said okay.

But then I started to wonder whether I'd made a mistake. Salvador *is* cute. And funny. And thoughtful . . . Anyway, the point is that it was too late to go back and change my mind— Salvador didn't seem interested in me anymore. So I'd been trying to forget about him. At least, to forget about him in *that way*. Not that it had been working.

So—now maybe, possibly, he *was* interested after all. But—how should I act? What should I do? I didn't know. This was too confusing!

I splashed more water on my face. *Get a grip, Elizabeth. You have bigger problems right now.* Problem number one being that on Saturday night, a whole lot of people were going to show up at our house.

The door opened, and I looked up.

It was Jessica.

Elizabeth

As soon as she saw me, I could tell she knew I knew.

"Don't kill me," were her first words.

I grabbed a paper towel, dried my face, and threw it into the wastebasket. "Are you nuts? How could you do this?"

"I didn't," Jessica protested. "Lacey invited a bunch of people and . . ."

"Lacey?"

"Yeah, Lacey. And Lila too. I don't know, it just sort of spiraled out of control."

"How many people do you think are coming?" I asked in a faint voice.

Jessica shrugged, and for the first time her face looked like she might be sick. "I don't know." She ran over to the sink, turned on the water, and splashed her own face—just like I had been splashing mine.

I grabbed a paper towel and handed it to her. She wiped her face and took some deep breaths. "Please don't chew me out, Elizabeth. You've got to help me. What am I going to do?"

I shook my head. "At this point I don't think there's any way we can stop it," I said. "So I guess we just better be prepared. How much is left of the grocery money Mom and Dad gave us?"

"About thirty dollars."

"We'll take that and our allowances and buy

as much soda and snack stuff as we can."

"What about Steven? As soon as he sees us bringing all that stuff in the house, he'll freak out."

"We'll hide it in our rooms and bring it down during the party."

"What if he hears about it at school or something?"

"He won't," I answered. "He's got basketball practice this afternoon, and tomorrow's Saturday. He usually just lounges around the house on Saturday. If anybody calls him, we'll say he's out. But what are we going to do when people start coming?"

"He's not going to tell people to go home," Jessica said. "He couldn't because some of his friends will be there. If he told people to leave, he'd look like a complete dork. He'll just have to go along with it and be a good sport."

"He might go along with it," I agreed. "I don't know about the good-sport part. But if we can convince him that the downstairs is going to be full of giggling girls playing loud music, he may stay upstairs all night. He'll never even know what's going on."

Jessica smiled. "So you think this is survivable?"

I nodded. "I think so. Yeah. But we'll need help."

Elizabeth

"Do you think Anna and Salvador would help us?" Jessica looked worried, and her lower lip began to tremble. I reached out and hugged her.

"Don't worry, Jess," I said. "They've already offered." I was relieved they had, even though the thought of hanging with Salvador suddenly made me feel a little . . . fluttery. I hoped I wouldn't come off as a totally weird, self-conscious freakazoid.

But I'd played dumb so far. I'd just keep playing dumb and hope things worked themselves out.

Wonder Girl.

Boy, was that a case of mistaken identity.

FRIDAY

1:30 P.M.: In the hall, five people Jessica doesn't recognize ask her about the party. Carried away by her sudden popularity, she gives them her address, then tells them to "bring all their friends."

1:45 P.M.: Elizabeth passes a note to Anna, explaining that the party is going to be huge and that she will need help buying refreshments.

1:46 P.M.: Lacey uses her study hall to photocopy flyers she has printed up promoting the "Wakefield Bonanza."

1:47 P.M.: Anna writes back to Elizabeth, saying that she knows where they can get lots of great snacks—cheap. The note is intercepted by Mrs. Pomfrey and read aloud to the entire class. Elizabeth sees several students make notations in their daily planners.

2:30 P.M.: At their locker Ronald Rheece asks Jessica about the party. Horrified, Jessica tries to pretend that she doesn't know what he is talking about, but Ronald assumes she is kidding and promises to be there with bells on. Jessica worries that he might mean that literally.

2:30 P.M.: Elizabeth comes up to Anna in the hall as she is excitedly discussing the party with Sheila Watson. Once Sheila leaves, Elizabeth asks Anna not to publicize the party too much. She explains that it is sort of a "covert mission" that has to be kept a secret from Steven.

3:30 P.M.: Salvador spots Gel in the grocery-store liquor aisle, putting beer into a cart. Salvador decides not to mention this to Elizabeth or Anna. After all, Gel isn't twenty-one. He'll get busted if he tries to buy alcohol. Hopefully.

Jessica

While Elizabeth and her crew shopped for refreshments, I went to the big discount store and bought about a thousand paper cups and napkins. I wasn't sure it was enough, but I couldn't buy any more because I didn't have any more money. Elizabeth had taken most of it to buy food.

I hoped we wouldn't run out of cups. But then again, maybe if we ran out of cups, people wouldn't drink as much soda. I had a horrible feeling that I'd made a mistake turning down all those offers to bring something.

I let myself in the front door and struggled up the stairs with the bags of cups and napkins. My room was already a disaster area. No place to put anything.

Elizabeth's room was in pretty good shape, so I decided to put the stuff in there. I dropped one of the bags on top of the desk and the other on the floor.

Between the bed and the wall, there was a big area of space that wouldn't show if you just stuck your head into the room—like Steven might do. The sodas and snacks could go there.

I heard some commotion outside. Elizabeth was back. I ran downstairs, looked out the front door, and started to laugh.

Elizabeth, Salvador, and Anna had three shopping carts piled up with sodas and bags of chips and popcorn.

Elizabeth brushed past me with her arms full of sacks. "Start taking stuff up. Salvador's got to take the carts back to the store."

"Think it'll be enough?" Salvador asked, beaming at me.

"I hope so. Looks like enough for six parties."

"Let's see how the first one goes, then we can talk about the other five," Anna said.

Salvador was looking through the sacks. "Let me take the bags with the soda," he said. "They're heavy. You guys take the ones with the chips and stuff." He handed Anna two grocery bags full of potato chips and crackers. Then he handed me two bags.

I headed back into the house and up the stairs. We piled the groceries in Elizabeth's room between the bed and the wall. When you stood in the hall-way and looked inside, you could barely see the tops of a few bags—which could have been anything. Nothing that would arouse suspicion.

Ten minutes later we were finished. Done. Squared away until it was time to start preparing for the party. We all stood outside on the sidewalk, making plans for tomorrow.

"I'll take these carts back to the store," Salvador said.

"I'll help you," Anna offered.

"No!" Salvador said quickly. "It's a long way. You go home. Hang out. Relax." He grinned. "Get some beauty sleep. I'll take these back, then I'll swing around your place tomorrow at about five. That'll put us here around five-thirty."

"Is that early enough?" Anna asked Elizabeth.

"I think so," Elizabeth said.

Anna grinned. "This is kind of fun. I feel like an undercover agent. Do you guys do this sort of thing very often?"

Elizabeth laughed and rolled her eyes. "Don't get me started. I could tell you stories you wouldn't believe."

"Don't tell them till Saturday 'cause I gotta move," Salvador said. He pushed the carts into each other and started hurtling down the street with the carts rattling.

"I should go too," Anna said. "Unless you need me to help you do something else."

"I think we've got it under control for now," Elizabeth told her. "Anna, thank you *so* much. You and Salvador are the best."

Anna smiled, lifted her hand in a good-bye wave, and then thrust it down into her pocket, walking off with her shoulders hunched.

I watched Anna disappear around the corner, thinking how lucky Elizabeth was to have a friend like her. I thought about my friends, like Lila. She was cool and a lot of fun, sure, but was she ever there for me when I needed her?

"What's the matter?" Elizabeth asked. "So far, so good. Why the long face?"

I shrugged. "I don't know. Suddenly I just feel kind of lonely."

Elizabeth grinned. "Wait till tomorrow night. You won't be lonely then."

"Think we'll get in trouble?" I asked, suddenly uneasy.

"How much trouble could we get into?" Elizabeth countered. "Steven can't ground us. And if we get everything cleaned up, Mom and Dad will never know."

I threw up my hands. "This is just too weird."

"What?"

"You. You're starting to sound like me."

"Uh-oh!" Elizabeth opened her mouth in mock horror.

"I'm serious. I'm starting to think you're more excited than I am."

"I *am* excited," Elizabeth admitted as we walked into the house. "But right now, I'm more worried about keeping Steven from killing us. When is he due home?"

"Soon."

"Okay. Our biggest problem is going to be the phone."

"Suggestions?"

"Change the answering machine so it picks up on the first ring. You know how lazy Steven is. He never answers the phone if he can help it. That way we're in total control of incoming calls."

"What if he calls somebody and they mention the party?" I asked.

"He had a practice today," Elizabeth said thoughtfully. "I'll bet if we have a nice, big starchy meal he'll nod off before we can get the dishes off the table. Let's have macaroni and cheese, garlic bread, and pound cake for dessert. That'll put him under. And he won't be calling anybody."

"You're a diabolical genius!" I gasped. My sister had certainly snapped out of lame mode.

"Just call me Wonder Girl," Elizabeth said with a giggle. "Come on, let's start the macaroni."

Salvador

I actually spent an hour on Saturday deciding what to wear. A record.

I wanted to look good, but I didn't want to look like I was *trying* to look good. Add to this the fact that I have what one might call a limited wardrobe, and you've got a fashion emergency.

I picked up a blue flannel shirt. "No," I said out loud.

No to the plain black T-shirt. No to the oxford button-down the Doña had given me. No to the Hanson-style ski sweater. No to Mr. Bubble.

No, no, *no!*

The fact was, I had a problem that went beyond clothing, and his name was Todd.

Elizabeth had said his name so casually, mentioned she was inviting an "old friend" to the party. But I could tell that there was something there. Who was he? A boyfriend? An ex-boyfriend? A crush? I mean, if he was such a good

79

"friend," why hadn't I ever heard of Todd before?

Todd. What kind of name was that? I bet he was some boring goody-goody. Why didn't he get a *normal* name—like Salvador Constantine Northern del Valle?

Yes, I had a feeling about Todd. A feeling called *jealousy*. I didn't know who he was or even whether he was interested in Elizabeth or anything.

Then again, how could he *not* be interested in Elizabeth?

And what if she was interested back?

I would *freak out* if that happened. It's one thing to have an unrequited crush on someone. It's another to have them date someone else right in front of your face. I just didn't think I could deal with that.

So tonight I wanted to look good. Because tonight was the night. I was going to come clean to Elizabeth. No more hinting around with comics. I was going to tell her that I thought she was the most wonderful person in the world. If I never said anything and then she started going out with someone else, I would spend my whole life wondering and never knowing if she could possibly ever like me back.

And that was why I was standing in the middle of my room in my underwear, unable to get dressed.

I finally gave up and pushed aside a pair of jeans to clear a space on my bed so I could sit down. *If I'm going to tell Elizabeth how I feel, I should practice,* I thought. *I don't want to come off like some loser.* "Elizabeth, I just want to tell you," I started. *No. Wait.* I tried again. "Elizabeth, there's something you should know." Hmmm. I cleared my throat and picked up a pillow. I pictured Elizabeth's face. "Elizabeth," I said. I imagined her smiling up at me, asking, "Yes, Salvador?" I knew exactly what I would say in that situation. Nothing at all. I leaned forward and gave my pillow a kiss—

"Salvador?"—just as my grandmother walked into my room.

Yikes! I jumped off the bed, then realized that I was still only in my underwear. I sat back down quickly, putting the pillow on my lap.

"Hi," I said, trying to sound casual.

The Doña stared at me. "I'll come back later," was all she said. Then she closed the door.

"Bye," I said faintly, then flopped back on the bed and slapped the pillow over my face. *This definitely makes the Humiliation Top Ten,* I thought. *Right up there with the time I barfed on Ms. Freeman, my third-grade teacher.*

I said a silent prayer that things would go better for me with Elizabeth tonight.

Salvador

I pulled the pillow off my face and turned to look at the clock. I had to choose something to wear soon. I was due over at Anna's in a few minutes. Next to the clock was a present I had bought for Anna yesterday—a little beanbag stuffed-animal thing, a pink pig. I had picked it up when I returned the shopping cart. The pig came with a tag that said its name was Care-y. It was kind of dorky, I guess, but I thought Anna would like it. Girls love that stuff.

I wanted to make sure that Anna was in a good mood at the party, and I figured a surprise would cheer her up. She had been acting a little strange when we shopped for the party food. I guessed that things were still kind of rough at home—that Tim was on Anna's mind a lot more than she was admitting. How could he not be when her mother was so sad all the time?

I wanted Anna to have a lot of fun and make friends tonight.

Maybe she could hang with *Todd* and keep him away from Elizabeth.

Hey. Maybe that could work out for both of us.

To Salvador

I remember kindergarten:
You ate my paste.

I remember second grade:
You made me a big red valentine.

I remember third grade:
You broke your arm in my backyard.

I have no memories without you.
I hope I never will.

A n n a

I decided I'd give Salvador the poem at the party instead of after. Maybe he and I could find a romantic spot somewhere, where we could hear music playing in the background, and I could give him the poem, and he would know.

He would know how I felt, I mean.

Ever since Salvador comforted me and then brought me that flower, I'd been paying closer attention to how things had changed between us. I had to admit, they'd been a bit strange lately, and I finally figured out why. Salvador had a crush on me. And I had a crush on him back.

It was *totally* weird to think about, but it was true. So I'd decided to make the first move. I knew Salvador would never say anything otherwise.

I rolled up the poem like a little scroll and tied it with some rattan ribbon.

The clock in the hall chimed. It was time to

get ready. I went into the bathroom and looked in the mirror. I'd never exactly been the glamorous type. I didn't have too much makeup.

But I did have a lipstick and an eyebrow pencil somewhere. I rummaged around in the bathroom drawer and located the lipstick and the pencil. I tested the pencil. It was soft enough to use as an eyeliner. Cool.

My brows are very thin and almost invisible. So I penciled in some really dramatic arched brows. Then I used the pencil to smudge a little black around the corners of my eyes like the models do in magazines.

I couldn't tell if I looked good or just weird. I wished there were someone I could ask. But my mom was having one of her bad days. Even on a good day she wouldn't qualify as a great judge of fashion and makeup.

I decided to keep going. If I chickened out, I could always wash it all off and go barefaced— my usual look.

The lipstick was a deep red. If I wasn't careful to get it on my lips exactly perfectly, I was going to look like Bozo the Clown.

I'd read some article about how to do this. Now, what had it said? Oh yeah. Do the V of your upper lip first.

I did that.

Okay.

Now fill in the rest.

My hand wasn't real steady, but I managed to get the red on my lips and nowhere else. The result was pretty spectacular.

I stared at myself. No wonder girls were so into this stuff. It was like, a miracle. I looked . . . well . . . I looked pretty.

I pulled my straight, black hair back into a ponytail and twisted it into a bun. There were some dusty hairpins down in the drawer. I didn't really know what I was doing, but I stuck a bunch of them in the bun. When I let go—it stayed. Amazing. Now for the clothes.

I'd looked through my wardrobe. I had some new jeans that fit great and were wide at the bottom. I dug around in my closet and found a short-sleeved, black velvet mock turtleneck, which I had worn last Christmas. I never get dressed up but decided, why not? I wanted to look good when I gave Salvador the poem, didn't I?

I stuck the lipstick in the pocket of my jeans and went to the front to wait for Salvador. He'd said he was coming by a little early.

Right on the dot (strange for Salvador), he rang the bell. When I answered it, he thrust this box wrapped up in beautiful paper at me.

"What is this?" I couldn't believe it. First flowers.

Anna

Now a present? *Salvador really* does *like me!*

"It's for you," he answered, coming in the front hall.

"For my birthday? That's not till next month."

"It's not for your birthday."

"Then what's it for?"

"Can't I bring you a present without getting the third degree?" He had this funny smile on his face. Like he was embarrassed and happy at the same time.

I took the package into the living room. The box was so beautiful, I hated to open it. The paper was soft yellow with big red roses. I would like to have wallpaper like that. It would be impossible to ever feel sad with wallpaper like that.

I carefully pulled the tape away from one side so I wouldn't tear the paper.

Salvador fidgeted impatiently. "Come on, Anna. Go for it."

"I want to save the paper."

"There's more paper where that came from. Live a little. Let 'er rip."

I tore the paper. It made a big, happy tearing sound, and I couldn't help laughing.

Salvador laughed too. Suddenly we were both laughing and giggling, and I wasn't even sure what we were laughing and giggling about.

I opened the box and pulled out an adorable little pink pig.

"Oh, he's so cute!" I flipped over the tag. "Care-y," I said. Suddenly I felt too shy to look Salvador in the face. *Care-y. He's telling me how much he cares about me.* A blush crept up my neck. And the pig was pink. Was that a coincidence, or was it supposed to be, like, a romantic color? I wasn't sure. "I love it," I said finally. "I just—" But I couldn't say any more because tears had flooded my eyes and I couldn't speak. Then I started crying. I mean *really* crying. Don't ask me what came over me, but suddenly I was just bawling.

Salvador looked panicked for a minute, like he might turn and run. But then he put his arm around my shoulders and patted my back. It was sort of awkward—but sweet. "Hey. I was trying to make you happy. I . . ."

"I am happy," I choked out. "I can't even tell you how happy I am."

"Well, if this is happy, I sure don't want to see you sad," he joked.

That made me laugh, and pretty soon I was over it. "I'm sorry." I sniffed, looking around the room for a tissue. "I don't know what made me do that."

Salvador smiled. "Hey! Don't worry." Then he looked at me and frowned. "Anna. There's something wrong with your face."

Anna

I ran to the mirror in the hall. Black eye pencil had smeared all over my face! It was so hilarious, I couldn't help bursting into laughter.

Salvador started laughing too. "I hope you didn't pay for that makeover," he teased. "If so, you need to ask for your money back."

I took the pig and headed for the bathroom. "Give me two minutes, and I'll be back out."

I went into the bathroom, washed my face, and did a little redo with the pencil. Then I put Care-y on my bed and gave him a pat on the head.

I went out into the hall, and Salvador broke into a big grin. "You look great, by the way. You'll be the prettiest girl there."

I grabbed my purse, looked inside, and saw the rolled-up poem. I almost changed my mind about giving it to him at the party. *Should I give it to him now?*

Nah, I decided. If he started bawling the way I had over the pig, we'd never get to Elizabeth's house.

Elizabeth

I was nervous all afternoon. At least the living room looked fabulous. It was full of streamers and balloons and paper flowers.

Steven wandered through a couple of times, and I kept waiting for some sign that he was getting suspicious. But if he thought there was an unusual amount of decorating going on for a girls' slumber party, he didn't say anything.

He spent most of the day sleeping. Around five he got dressed and announced that he was going to the video store to pick up some stuff to watch.

I had a sudden anxiety attack that he might run into somebody at the video store who would mention the party. "Want me to go?" I asked quickly.

Steven gave me this funny look. "Why are you offering to go?"

"We need some more soda," I croaked. "It's on the way."

Elizabeth

Steven shrugged. "Okay. Great. Let me write down the movies I want."

Ten minutes later I was on my way to the video store with a list of five movies to rent for Steven. Fortunately they were all action-adventure movies. That meant the sound track would be loud enough to drown out a lot of the party noise.

It took only a couple of minutes at the store to locate all the films, and when I was checking out I saw Cathy Connors, Steven's girlfriend, standing in the other line.

I waved, and she waved back. But she had a funny look on her face.

I realized the line had moved and it was my turn to check out. By the time I was finished, Cathy was gone, and I didn't have a chance to say anything to her. Not that I *could* have said anything about the party.

I hurried home as fast as I could and saw Anna and Salvador coming up the street.

"Hi!" Anna said. "We're here to help. What do you need us to do?"

"I don't suppose you could chloroform Steven and lock him in the basement for the next few hours?" I asked.

"Hey! Everybody likes a good party," Salvador said with a laugh. "Why don't you just invite him?"

"With any luck, Steven won't even know we're having one," I answered wryly. Then I looked at Anna and did a double take. She looked gorgeous. Like a model!

"You look great," I said happily.

"Thanks," Anna said. "I'm jazzed for this party."

We all went inside. There was a box of CDs on the floor. "You guys start picking out music. I'm going to run upstairs and get dressed."

I ran up the stairs just in time to see Steven come stalking out of Dad's den. His face looked *furious*. Uh-oh. My heart stopped. Had somebody clued Steven in?

Steven saw me and threw his hands in the air. "Cathy Connors is insane!" he yelled.

I didn't know what to say to that, so I just smiled nervously.

"I called her to see if she wanted to come over and watch movies with me, but before I could get two words out of my mouth, she accused me of breaking a date with her because I was having a party and had asked somebody else to be my date. Can you believe that?"

I swallowed. This was going to be hard to explain.

"She's nuts," Steven went on to say. "I told her I wasn't having a party—that you and Jessica

93

were. Then she said that wasn't true because she saw you renting videos at the store and you wouldn't be renting videos if you were having a party. So it's obvious, she says, that I am having a party. And furthermore, everybody knows about it because she's heard people talking about it. So I explained they were *my* movies, but she wouldn't listen and called me a liar!"

"Well, uhhhhh."

Steven shook his head. "Where does she get these ideas?"

Fortunately he wasn't really expecting an answer. He snatched the bag of movies and stalked off to the den.

I ran into my room, jumped into a new pair of cargo pants and a pullover, and hurried into the bathroom.

Jessica was in there with the full arsenal. Hot rollers, blow-dryer, curling iron, foundation, blush, lipsticks, brushes, and a lot of little metal devices that looked like something they might have used to torture people during the Inquisition.

"I hate to tell you this, but we have a problem with Steven."

"*What?*" Jessica dropped the curling iron, and it fell on her foot. "*Ouch!*"

I dove for the iron and managed to snag it before it set the house on fire. "Cathy Connors heard about the party, called Steven, and accused him of breaking a date with her because she thinks that it's his party and he asked somebody else to be his date."

Jessica lifted her foot and stuck her burned toe under the faucet. She grimaced as the cold water washed over it. "So what did Steven say?"

"He thinks she's nuts."

"Great!" Jessica pulled her foot out of the sink and beamed. "So there's no problem."

"It's not great! He'll eventually find out the truth, and he'll be doubly mad that we got him into a fight with his girlfriend."

Jessica picked up a brush and pulled it through her hair. "They'll make up. They always do."

There was no point in trying to talk to Jessica when she was in Beautyville. We'd just have to make it up to Steven later.

I slapped on some lip gloss and ran a brush through my hair. Downstairs, the doorbell rang.

Jessica and I froze. The first guests were arriving.

"Well?" I said. "Do you want to get it? Or do you want me to?"

Jessica leaned over and let her blond hair hang down. Then she flipped her head back so that her hair splayed out over her shoulders. "I'll get it."

She drooped her shoulders, stuck out her

pelvis, and started to slouch out of the bathroom.

"Why are you walking like that?" I asked.

She gave me a dirty look. "It's supposed to make me look cool."

"Well, it doesn't. It makes you look like an idiot. And if you don't move it, whoever's at the door is going to give up and go home."

"Ha, ha!" Jessica said. She hurried into her room, which looked like it had been hit by a bomb, and stepped into some brown leather mules.

The doorbell rang again.

"Hurry!" I urged. "If you don't answer it, Steven might."

That did it. Jessica shot toward the door, and I heard her thundering down the steps.

I went back into my room and rustled around in the bags for more chips and stuff. It was time to start putting things out.

Did we need more cups downstairs? I wondered. Probably not yet. The big paper bag full of cups and napkins was still on my desk. That was fine for now.

I poked my head out the door to make sure Steven wasn't in the hall. He wasn't, and I hurried down the steps.

Salvador and Anna had put on some dance music, and they were looking through piles of old albums that had belonged to my parents when they were in college.

"Some of this vintage stuff is good," Salvador said. "Okay if we play it?"

"Sure, as long as we don't scratch the records. My father is slightly fanatical about his albums. Who came?" I asked.

"Brian Rainey and Kristin," Anna answered. "They're in the kitchen with Jessica."

I went into the kitchen. Brian had brought a sack of ice, and they were trying to decide where to put it. "There's a tin tub in the garage," I suggested.

"That would work," Brian said.

"I'll show you." Jessica led Brian out the back door, and I could hear the two of them talking and laughing on the way to the garage.

Kristin turned to me. "Jessica said not to bring anything, but I made this mixed tape that I thought we could play. It has lots of good dance music. Do you mind if I put it on?"

"Sounds great," I told her. "The stereo's in the living room."

Kristin went into the living room, and a few seconds later Salvador came into the kitchen. "Anna and Kristin are talking like old friends," he said, beaming. "Anna actually told Kristin her secret for applying lipstick—can you believe it?"

Elizabeth

I felt my mouth drop open. "Really? That seems so un-Anna."

He smiled and looked at me from beneath his thick lashes. "I never know *what* she's going to do."

Noticing his lashes gave me another funny bump in my stomach.

"What can I do?" he asked, looking around the kitchen.

"Help me put some of these out." I opened the refrigerator and looked at all the dips Jessica and I had made the day before. Salvador stood behind me and looked over my shoulder. He was standing so close, I could feel his breath on the back of my neck.

Little butterflies fluttered up and down my spine, and I suddenly felt shy. I turned around and started to say something about finding a tray, but the words never came out.

We were face-to-face. Just inches apart. He was looking right into my eyes. And I was looking into his.

I kept waiting for him to step back. Or to say something. Or to crack a joke and break the tension. Instead he leaned forward a bit. He smelled fresh and clean, like fabric softener.

"Is Todd going to help set up?" he asked.

What is he talking about? I felt dizzy. "Who?"

Salvador smiled. "Elizabeth," he said.

Both of us jumped when the back door opened and Jessica and Brian came bursting in. Their laughter seemed incredibly loud. The lights seemed too bright. The ice glittered. The spell was broken.

"Want me to start filling some glasses with soda?" Brian asked.

"I'll do that," Salvador said quickly, hurrying away from me and toward the table. I didn't know how to feel. Disappointed? Relieved?

"Okay, should I make the punch, then?" Brian suggested. "I have the family recipe."

I managed a laugh. "Knock yourself out," I said. "Here's some ginger ale and some fruit-drink mix."

"What is this?" Jessica demanded. She examined the label on the drink mix. "Elizabeth! Did you have to get the *generic* brand?"

"It was on *sale*," I explained. I swear! Didn't Jessica understand that we had to stick to a budget? Anyone would think that the Pentagon was paying for this party. "And it's just for the punch. We've got sodas too."

"It'll be good," Salvador promised. "Sparkling fruit punch."

Jessica gave him a dubious look, but Brian went ahead and poured the soda over the ice in the bowl. Then he added some of the powdered fruit stuff and stirred it with a wooden spoon.

"Who will be the first to taste Brian's Famous Packs-a-Punch?" Brian asked. He looked at Jessica and waggled his eyebrows.

She peered at the bright pink liquid. "I'll try it," she said hesitantly.

He ladled some into a glass. "Here you go."

Jessica took a sip, then spat it back into the glass. "Ugh!" she said, sticking out her tongue. "This is *disgusting*." Salvador cracked up. "That is not funny, El Salvador," Jessica insisted.

"Hmmm." Brian frowned over the punch bowl. "I guess I'd better fiddle with the recipe."

"Good luck," Jessica said, wiping her mouth out with a napkin. Her tongue was fluorescent pink.

Maybe the generic brand *had* been a mistake.

Salvador laughed again, and I looked over at him. Our eyes met, and he held my gaze for a moment.

I swallowed hard and looked at the floor.

You can make it through this party, I told myself. *You can act normal around Salvador for the next few hours.*

I really wished I could believe it.

Top Ten Excuses Given to Parents
by Kids Going to the Wakefield Party

10. The library has a new twenty-four-hour policy.
 9. Of *course* their parents will be there!
 8. Emergency chess club meeting.
 7. It's just a bunch of kids, Mom. How crazy can it get?
 6. Need to practice social skills for college interviews.
 5. But Jennie's mom said it was okay for *her* to go!
 4. All-night study session for algebra exam.
 3. Jessica Wakefield is stuck in a well!
 2. You're always saying I should get out more.
 1. Party? What party?

Jessica

The doorbell rang again, and I rushed to answer it.

"Hi!" I said with my brightest smile as I flung the door wide.

"Hi, Jessica!" Ronald Rheece chirped.

I stood there, frozen in horror.

"May I come in?" he asked.

"Uh," I said, trying to think of some excuse to keep him out of my party. Just what I needed was for it to turn into Dork Central. But just then Kristin came up behind me.

"Oh, hi, Ronald," she said. "Would you like a soda?"

Kristin could be too friendly for her own good.

"Sure," Ronald said, and brushed past me. *Maybe he'll stay in the kitchen all night,* I thought hopefully. *Or maybe he'll tell Lila and Lacey that he's my best friend and ruin my life.*

I groaned and started to close the door.

"Jessica!" Lila called from the end of the walk.

"Hi!" I said.

She gave me an air kiss and swept in like some kind of supermodel. Roary Michaels was on her arm. Ashlee, Courtnee, and Maree tagged along behind.

"Hi, Jessee!" Ashlee said brightly, as if she were my friend instead of my replacement.

I gritted my teeth but managed not to vomit. "How are you?" I said.

Maree smiled. "We are, like, so—"

"Incredibly ready to party!" Courtnee finished. "We brought you these—"

"Little chocolate candy thingies," Maree said. "Ashlee's mom makes them, and they are, like—"

"The best. The absolute best—you won't even believe it!" Courtnee looked like she might die of joy over the fact that they brought candy. It *was* nice, I had to admit. Still, that didn't mean I wanted to talk to them.

"Thanks so much," I said. "Why don't you put those candies in a bowl? There's some in the kitchen."

"Okay," Courtnee said.

"See you, Jessee," Ashlee added. And the Double E's wandered off, squealing to each other.

Lila stayed with me in the front entrance, a small smile on her face.

"I'm so glad you're here!" I told her, managing

to turn her so that she was facing the dining room—where Brian and Salvador could be seen putting out food and glasses full of soda. I wanted her to see that we already had some guys at our party.

"Roary," Lila said dramatically. "This is Jessica Wakefield, Steven Wakefield's sister."

Roary was pretty handsome, with shoulder-length brown hair and a friendly smile. "Where's Stevo?" he asked.

Stevo? Since when did people call Steven "Stevo"?

"Yes," Lila said. "Where *is* Stevo?" Like she and Steven were tight.

Just what I needed was Lila going to look for my brother. "Well," I hedged.

"Roar-inacious!" bellowed some enormous guy who had just walked through the front door. He picked Roary up and swung him around. Three other huge, jockish-looking guys were behind him. They all started thumping each other on the back and saying, "What's up, man?" and "How's it goin'?" and other guylike stuff. Lila just stood there, beaming. "I'm so glad you guys could make it," she said to the guys. Like it was *her* party.

The guys pounded fists—a couple of them even high-fived Lila—and headed into the living room. I smiled after them. *I'll meet them later,* I thought. *I'm sure Lila will introduce me.*

"Okay, so, like, where should we put this?" Ashlee asked the other EE's as she walked back into the dining room with a bowl full of candies.

"On the dining-room table?" Maree suggested. "Or maybe—"

"In the living room," Courtnee interrupted. "Maybe someone's hungry."

All three girls giggled, and they put the bowl down right in front of Ronald Rheece, who was sitting on the couch.

He took a candy and popped it in his mouth. His eyes opened wide. "Wow!" He reached for another.

"Don't eat them *all,*" Courtnee said, kind of rudely. I was annoyed that she was being mean to one of my guests, even if he was just my nerdy locker partner. But before I could step in and say something, she wandered away to talk to Roary's friends.

Somebody turned up the music. Suddenly the volume on the party had gone up. Way up. People were talking and laughing so loudly, I couldn't believe Steven hadn't noticed. But even if he did—we were past the point of no return. People were streaming through the front door.

I smiled and said, "Hi," as a group of six people walked past. "Come on in."

"Who was that?" Lila wanted to know.

"No idea," I said.

The place was getting packed, but not a single person was dancing yet—I guess nobody wanted to be first.

I grabbed Lila's hand. "Come on, let's get the dancing started!" I suggested. But before I could drag her and Roary into the living room, Lacey walked through the front door with Gel and the rest of her entourage.

"Hi," Lacey said—*to Roary*. She didn't even acknowledge Lila.

Roary smiled back. "Hi." Then he nodded at Gel. It was the kind of brisk nod that guys give each other when they have to be polite but don't like each other very much. Gel gave Roary a cool look.

Lila was looking over her shoulder, not acknowledging Lacey either.

Man, it was getting chilly in there. *It's up to me to break the ice,* I decided. *Just call me Madame Ambassador. Using my powers of cool to unite the popular people of Sweet Valley.* "Lacey Frells, meet Lila Fowler."

At that point Lila and Lacey actually went so far as to exchange frosty smiles.

Lacey leaned against Gel's arm. "This is Gel. And these are Gel's friends, Danny, Marlon, and Chris."

Danny was kind of cute. But Marlon and Chris looked like thugs.

"Is there any food?" Chris asked. What a charmer.

"Lots of it," I answered. "In the dining room."

Chris, Marlon, and Danny ambled away. That left Lila, Lacey, Gel, Roary, and me all standing in a cozy little group.

"So!" I said to Lacey in a bright voice. "You and Lila have a lot in common."

Lacey lifted a brow like she wasn't sure that was a compliment, and then she gave Lila a rude, head-to-toe stare. "Oh, really? Like what?"

Lila colored angrily and returned the head-to-toe stare. "I can't imagine."

Uh-oh. This wasn't going well. Now that I stopped to think about it, they really didn't have much in common except that they were both popular and could be obnoxious. But I couldn't say that. "You're both very into fashion," I said. It was totally lame, but it was all I could come up with.

Lila looked at Lacey's black tank and stretch pants and frowned, as if to say she didn't consider Lacey's outfit particularly fashionable.

Lacey caught the look, and her eyes narrowed. "I guess . . . but I've never been that crazy about the country-club-dork look."

Lila looked shocked. "I bought this skirt at a runway show. In Paris."

Lacey threw back her head and gave a big belly laugh. Right in Lila's face. "*You* bought it? Or *Daddy* did? Did he buy that perky little nose too?" Then she put a possessive hand on Gel's arm and they walked away.

Lila turned to me. "Was that a friend of yours?"

I shook my head. "Hardly." Oh, well. So *don't* call me Madame Ambassador. "I'm sorry about that, Lila."

She shrugged. "People at SVJH certainly are different," she said.

That was for sure. I was glad I had my old friends around again. Lila would never have been as obnoxious as Lacey was—they were *totally* different. I was so glad to be hanging with my old crowd again.

"Do you want something to drink, Lila?" Roary asked.

Lila batted her eyelashes. "Isn't he sweet?" she asked me. "I'll go with you, Roary. Are you coming, Jess?"

"In a few." I really wanted to stay by the door and see who else showed up.

Lila gave a wave, and she and Roary made their way into the crowd.

A moment later Elizabeth and Salvador were

at my elbow. "How's it going?" Elizabeth asked.

"Great," I told her. "There's a lot of people here, but we don't seem to be out of control or any—" Elizabeth's eyes had gone wide. "What?" I turned to look behind me.

"Hi, Jessica." It was Aaron Dallas—my sort-of ex. He was just as cute as ever.

"Aaron!" I hugged him. "I didn't know you were coming!"

I turned to look at the guy next to him and realized why Elizabeth had gone bug-eyed. Aaron had come with Todd Wilkins—*Elizabeth's* ex.

"Hi, Todd," she said in a small voice.

Naturally, I turned to see how Salvador was reacting to all of this. He had turned a sickly shade of green.

"Elizabeth, dude, what's up?" Todd asked.

Dude? That's weird. Todd was the kind of guy who always spoke in complete sentences. I cast a sideways glance at Elizabeth. She looked dazed.

"Um, not much. This is Salvador." Elizabeth looked up at him, and Salvador smiled. It wasn't his normal grin, though. He looked pretty tense.

"Hi," Salvador said.

"'Sup, dude?" Todd held up his hand, like he was going for a high five. He looked like an idiot. Elizabeth always did have horrible taste in guys.

Elizabeth stared at him a moment. "So, Todd," she said finally. "Read any good books lately?"

I rolled my eyes. Like I wanted to stand there listening to the fifty works of Shakespeare Todd had picked up over the summer.

"No." Todd shook his head. "Aaron and I have been playing tons of basketball. I hardly have any time to read."

So Mr. Intellectual has become a jock? My mouth fell open a little. *Well, at least I won't have to stand here and listen to Todd and Elizabeth discuss literature, like I used to. But what could Elizabeth possibly have to say to a Todd who doesn't read?*

Elizabeth flashed me a rescue-me glance.

I cleared my throat. "Todd, Aaron, let's go get a drink. I'm thirsty."

Aaron offered his elbow. "Shall we?" he asked, wiggling his eyebrows.

I giggled and put my arm through his. "We shall." I waved at Elizabeth. "See you later!" And Aaron, Todd, and I headed for the crowded living room, where everyone was talking, dancing, eating, and laughing. At *my* party.

No doubt about it . . . this was getting good.

8:46 P.M.: Jessica discovers a broken lamp in the corner of the living room. She puts it in the broom closet, assuming Steven will never, ever look in there.

8:48 P.M.: Jessica discovers a fluorescent pink punch stain on the living-room drapes. She folds the fabric so the stain doesn't show.

8:49 P.M.: Roary's jock friends begin playing a game of touch football with a throw pillow.

8:50 P.M.: Jessica discovers a smoldering cigarette between the couch cushions.

8:51 P.M.: Salvador finally manages to get Elizabeth alone in the hallway. He is just about to tell her how he feels about her when Jessica runs up and begs Elizabeth to help her do something about the couch.

8:53 P.M.: Aaron fumbles the pillow and Todd retrieves it, scoring a touchdown against the bookshelf. Two of

Roary's friends pick him up and carry him around the living room on their shoulders in celebration.

8:58 P.M.: Elizabeth goes to the broom closet to get the fire extinguisher. "I can explain that," Jessica says when she sees Elizabeth staring at the broken lamp.

9:06 P.M.: Anna locates Salvador. She has her poem in hand. Just as she is about to give him the poem, a couch pillow beans Salvador in the head, causing him to spill soda all over her. He promises to return with paper towels. Todd apologizes to Anna profusely.

9:13 P.M.: Elizabeth douses the couch with the fire extinguisher. Jessica flips the cushions over. "There," she says brightly. "Good as new." Elizabeth says a silent prayer that their parents will agree.

Jessica

More people poured through the front door. One guy who didn't look at all familiar walked right up to me. "Hey, babe," he said. "What's up? My name's Jeff."

Who did this guy think he was? "Hi, Jeff," I said coolly. "You know, most girls don't really like to be called 'babe.' Because of the pig reference."

He opened his eyes wide. "I didn't mean—"

"There's food in the living room," I cut him off. "Have fun!" I turned my back on him. *Get lost, Mr. Smooth.*

I turned and found myself face-to-face with Bethel. "Hi!" I said.

"Hey, Jessica." Bethel smiled. "This is some party," she said, looking around the room. Then she frowned. I followed her gaze and saw Lacey standing in a corner with Gel, a sneer on her face.

I bit my lip. Were those two going to be at each other's throats all night? I hoped not. After all, Lacey had already been rude to Lila—what would stop her from messing with Bethel?

"I guess I'd better steer clear of that," Bethel said quietly. She looked at me. "I don't want to cause any problems for you."

I let out a relieved sigh. "Thanks, Bethel. That's cool of you." It actually *was* really cool. I knew Lacey wouldn't have thought twice about ruining my evening.

"Well," Bethel said, "I think I'm going to hit the dance floor. See you later."

"See you, Bethel." I watched her disappear into the crowd. The party was really hopping, and I was queen of the scene. So what if a couple of things had gotten broken? That was supposed to happen at a party, right? When your friends come over, they're allowed to get a little rowdy.

A bitter smell made my nose sting.

Smoke. Somebody had lit another cigarette.

As if on cue, Elizabeth appeared at my elbow. "Some guys are smoking in the dining room. What are we going to do?"

"Nothing," I whispered. "We can't exactly tell them to stop."

"Mom and Dad will smell it when they get home," she said. I rolled my eyes. Did Elizabeth *have* to be so uptight? "Even if they don't notice the couch."

"Not if we leave the doors open all day tomorrow.

Relax." I peered into the living room. Unbelievable! It was *packed.* I saw Gel go over to the sound system and start fiddling with it. Suddenly the music went off. The crowd began to boo. *I'd better get in there and see what he's doing,* I thought.

I started to walk toward Gel, but Elizabeth grabbed my elbow. "We have another problem. Ronald Rheece ate an entire bowl of chocolates and now he won't stop jumping on the couch."

"What?" I screeched.

At that moment music came blasting out of speakers. It was so loud, I could actually feel my teeth vibrating. What a jerk—*what was Gel doing to our sound system?*

I saw Ronald's head bob above everyone else's. "I love this song!" he yelled.

The crowd cheered, and suddenly everyone started moving. The entire party was jumping and dancing.

Lila and the Double E's were busting a move in the living room with a bunch of guys I didn't know. Lacey and Gel were bumping and grinding in the corner. Suddenly Ronald climbed onto the back of the couch.

"Courtnee!" he screamed. "Here I come!"

My heart sank as he dove into the crowd. *I'm going to die of embarrassment,* I thought. But the crowd just passed him over their heads until he landed in the middle of the dance floor.

Then Ronald started getting down. When I realized that he was going to *dance*, I was so horrified that I cringed and actually put my hands over my eyes.

But when I didn't hear deafening laughter, I took my hands away. Nobody was paying Ronald any attention. Everyone was too busy grooving.

"I don't believe this," Elizabeth said, wide-eyed.

"All right!" I pushed my way into the middle of the dance floor. Finally even Elizabeth joined in. This really *was* the party of the semester.

It was an out-and-out rave!

That's when I saw Steven.

A n n a

"Hi," I said to the cool-looking girl next to me.

"*What?*" she yelled over the music.

"*Hi,*" I repeated, louder this time. "I'm Anna. What's your name?" We were standing next to a speaker, and I could hardly hear my own voice.

The girl nodded and looked at her watch. "*Nine-thirty,*" she shouted.

So much for making conversation. *Be friendly,* said a voice in my head. *Make an effort, and people will be nice back.* This had always been my brother's advice on how to make friends. Why had it always worked for him and not for me?

A party was not a good place to start remembering Tim. I pushed thoughts of him out of my mind and tried to concentrate on the scene around me. I wished someone would ask me to dance. Brian and Kristin looked like they were having a great time. Even Bethel, who hardly ever cuts loose, was dancing with this way-cute high-school boy.

Anna

So—where was Salvador?

After all, wasn't I supposed to be Anna Cinderella Wang tonight? Then why was I pressed against the wall, watching Jessica Wakefield shake her groove thing with Ronald Rheece? This most definitely was not my idea of the perfect party night.

I was standing there with my arms folded across my chest when Jeff Federman came over to me.

"Hey, babe. What's up?" he shouted in my ear. *"My name's Jeff."*

I stared at him. "No kidding, Jeff," I said. "Like I could forget that time in fifth grade when we played Three Minutes in the Closet and you totally had Cool Ranch Dorito breath." Let me tell you, Jeff Federman was imprinted indelibly in my brain.

He seemed shocked. *"Anna?"* he asked, like I had risen from the dead or something. Didn't he recognize me? "You look . . ." He looked me up and down as he searched for the right word. "Better."

Better? Was that supposed to be a *compliment*? "You don't," I told him.

He walked away. Big loss.

I was starting to feel pretty sure that this *wasn't* going to be the night of my life after all. I thought about my poem to Salvador. Maybe that would salvage things. I wasn't really in the mood to give it to him anymore, though.

But I knew that would change once I saw him again. I moved away from the speaker.

Some jock guy came up to me. He was huge. I guessed he was on the high-school football team. "Will you come outside with me?" he asked.

This made me nervous. "Why?"

"I have a bet with my buddies over there." He gestured at three guys across the room. One of them waved to me. "Ten bucks says I can jump over your head."

I couldn't take it anymore. I was going to find Salvador.

"Sorry," I told the guy. "Maybe next party."

I pushed my way through the crowd. It was tough. Lots of the high-school kids were tall, and it was hard to see over them.

Finally I reached the kitchen. No Salvador. Maybe he was outside. I went out the back door. Little knots of people stood around, talking. I didn't see Salvador, so I walked along the drive that ran along the side of the house.

A movement to the left attracted my attention. I recognized the silhouette. It was Lacey. She was standing with a couple of Gel's friends. They were smoking. I guess the two guys had finished because they threw their cigarette butts into the bushes. Wasn't she going to say anything to them? They could burn down the house! I thought she was supposed to be Jessica's friend.

"Stop that!" I shouted.

The two guys turned and looked at me. One of them laughed. "Are you going to make me?"

I had to admit—he had a point. The guy was at least twice my size. "Just show some *respect*," I said, staring hard at Lacey. These guys were really her responsibility. It was her they would listen to, not me.

Lacey just rolled her eyes and tossed the cigarette she was smoking into the bushes with the others.

Why did I bother? I turned and headed back into the party just as Bethel busted through the back door with one of Gel's friends. They were both laughing.

"Hi, Anna!" Bethel said when she saw me. "Do you know Danny?"

Danny gave a low bow. "It is a pleasure to meet you," he said in a debonair voice. Bethel laughed, and even I managed a smile.

"How do you two know each other?" I asked, slightly confused. Danny was in high school, I knew that much.

"The jock connection," Bethel explained. "Danny and my older sister used to run together before she left for college."

Danny grinned. "Us jocks have to stick together. We can't drink or smoke, so at a party sometimes you need a fresh-air partner."

I nodded. Of course. It *had* been getting smoky inside.

"Danny!" a voice called. Bethel looked toward the speaker, then rolled her eyes. It was Lacey, of course.

"Hey, Lacey!" Danny said. "Hey, Chris. Marlon." Danny gave the guys a small wave.

Lacey strode over to us. "Hi, *Bethel.*" Lacey said Bethel's name like it was an insult. "I see you finally managed to get out of your house for once. Why don't you come join us, Danny?" She nodded toward Gel's other friends.

Bethel sucked in her breath, and I saw her jaw muscles working. Danny looked from Lacey, to Bethel, then at me, as if to say, *What's going on?* Finally Bethel just shrugged, like she had decided something. "It's good to see you too, Lacey," she said.

Lacey rolled her eyes. "I never said it was good—"

"Let's go inside, Bethel," I suggested. *Shut up, Lacey,* I thought. I was sick of her.

Bethel looked at me for a long moment. "Good idea," she said. She turned to Danny. "See you later."

"I'll come with you," he volunteered. I looked over at Lacey, whose mouth had dropped open. I tried not to smile. Danny was obviously a cool guy—with good taste in girls.

Which reminded me of why I had come outside in the first place. To find my cool guy—Salvador.

"See you, Lacey," Danny said as we walked through the back door. She didn't even respond.

For the first time at this party, I was starting to have a good time.

Jessica

Steven yanked me into Mom's office. He closed the door so we could hear each other.

"I'm going to kill you," he said calmly.

I smiled sheepishly. "Can you wait until tomorrow?"

"I'm serious, Jessica. How could you do this?"

"Steven! It's just a party. And a lot of those people are your friends. What's the big deal?"

"The big deal is I didn't know anything about it. And I talked to Mom and Dad this morning and promised them that everything was under control! You do realize that they're going to blame *me* for this, don't you?"

Wow. Steven was right. He was going to be in huge trouble if our parents ever found out about this party.

What a lucky break! That meant he could *never* tell on me.

"Besides," he went on angrily, "I told Cathy you were having a slumber party. And now she

125

thinks this is my party and that for some reason I didn't want her to come."

That was pretty bad, and I felt kind of awful about it. "Want me to talk to her?" I offered. "We could call her right now. I could explain everything."

"No," Steven shouted. "You've caused enough trouble already. Look, I'm going up to the den to call Cathy and try to convince her that I'm not the biggest jerk in Sweet Valley. And I want you to make sure this crowd clears out by midnight."

"But . . ."

"But nothing. If you don't clear them out, I will."

I folded my arms across my chest. "You're actually going to tell Roary Michaels and a whole bunch of people you know from school that they have to leave because it's past your bedtime?"

Steven looked so angry, I thought he might explode. His face turned purple, and a little vein in his head began to throb. "You are a blackmailer. You know that?"

"I'm just trying to put things in perspective for you," I said. Big Bad Brother didn't scare me at all—there was no way I was telling all of those people who had come to *my* party to go home!

Steven garbled something unintelligible about how he was going to kill me and then stalked out and up the stairs.

I didn't know if he would be back or not. And I didn't care.

I headed out of Mom's office and over to the drinks on the dining-room table. I grabbed a cup of punch and took a sip.

Gross!

I spat my drink back into my cup. Was it my imagination, or was the punch even worse than it had been before? I tasted it again. Alcohol. The punch was spiked.

Great. Just what I needed was for kids to start getting drunk and rowdy. Hopefully the punch was too vile for anyone to drink it.

But what was I going to do? I had to get Elizabeth.

I headed toward the front of the house. Just as I passed the front door, the doorbell rang. I yanked it open, ready to tell whoever it was to just go home.

Oh no. I nearly slammed the door, but that would have been a very bad idea. Because the people on the front step weren't party guests. They were *police!* With blue uniforms, badges, and everything. Their lips were moving, but I couldn't hear a word they were saying. *"Just a minute!"* I yelled.

I ran into the living room, elbowed my way through the crowd, and turned off the CD.

People began to boo.

"Quiet!" I shouted. Then I ran back to the front

door. "I'm sorry," I said, trying to sound calm. I batted my eyelashes. "Is there a problem?"

"May we come in?" one of the officers asked. He was tall and bald. His partner was short and kind of round, with glasses and a silver mustache.

"Um. Sure." I let them in, my heart pounding.

As soon as we walked into the living room, a tense hush fell over the party.

"Whose home is this?" Baldie asked.

Where was Elizabeth when I needed her? "Mine," I squeaked.

Mustache gave me an even look. "Where are your parents?"

"Um. They're—out?" I answered. *I'm dead meat.*

"We've had a complaint about the noise," Baldie went on. "If you're having a party of this size, you're supposed to have a permit and inform your neighbors."

Right. I hadn't even informed my *brother.* If the police told my parents about this, I could kiss my future good-bye. I had to think of something, and it had to be quick. "A . . . *party?*" I repeated in an amazed tone. Then I started to laugh. "You think this is a party?"

The policemen looked around. "I would say it is a party. Yes," Mustache said.

"Oh no," I said, doing my best wide-eyed-and-innocent act. "No, no, no, no, *no.* This is actually the cast of *Rave,* a new teen musical. We're the drama club, and we're working on an . . . improv piece. We didn't mean to break any laws or anything."

Finally, out of the corner of my eye, I caught sight of Elizabeth. She looked like she was about to faint.

Mustache surveyed the room. "Drama club?" He looked back at me and cocked an eyebrow.

Brian Rainey stepped forward. "Yes, sir. This is our big musical number." I let out a breath. Thank goodness *someone* was backing me up.

"It's the showstopper," Kristin added, standing next to Brian. "Would you like us to perform it for you?"

Perform? Okay, now we were getting a little overboard.

Mustache looked like he wasn't buying a word of it. But he did give us an amused smile. "Oh, the *musical* number," he said. "No, I don't think we need to see that." He looked around the room. "Just keep the noise down," he said to the crowd. Then he turned back to me. "Young lady, if my partner and I have to come back here again, the cast of *Rave* is going to be written up in a citation. Do you understand me?"

I nodded. "Thank you, sir," I said quietly.

Brian followed them toward the door. "If you

change your mind, there's a matinee on Sunday."

Baldie gave an enough-already wave, and the policemen got in the car and pulled away from the curb.

Like they say, policemen are your friends.

Brian came over, picked me up, and swung me around, laughing.

A cheer went up and people were patting me on the back, giving me the thumbs-up sign, and stamping their feet. Even Lila and Roary and his crew were smiling and applauding.

The only person who didn't look thrilled was Elizabeth.

Elizabeth

"It's okay," Salvador said softly. "They're gone." He put his hands over mine to stop them from shaking. They felt warm and strong. But when I saw Jessica heading toward us, I felt embarrassed and pulled my hands away.

"Elizabeth!" Todd elbowed his way through the crowd.

I smiled. Good old Todd. He had been acting weird before, but he still wanted to check up on me and make sure I was okay.

"Dude." Todd clapped Jessica on the shoulder. "That was so funny!"

Funny? I couldn't believe this! Had Todd gotten a personality transplant or something? What was the matter with him? Couldn't he be a little more considerate? Like—well, like Salvador, for example.

"Piece of cake," Jessica said with a pleased smile.

She looked so smug, I just wanted to kick her. "Do you realize how much trouble we're going to be in if Mom and Dad find out?" I demanded.

"Why would they find out?"

"Right," I said, my voice dripping sarcasm. "Why would they possibly find out just because the police were here? And look. Gel's over by the sound system again. That couldn't possibly cause a problem."

That got to her—Jessica looked worried. "If Gel is in charge of the music again, we really *will* be in trouble. Listen, would you please go upstairs and see if you can find some mellow music? Ask Steven. He's got a lot of nice romantic stuff. And when you get back, there's another minor situation with the punch I need to discuss with you."

"Where is Steven?" I asked.

"Probably in his room. He was going to call Cathy, explain everything, and ask her to come over."

"Okay," I said, heading for the stairs. I turned to Todd. "See you later." Although I hoped I wouldn't.

"I'll come with you, Elizabeth," Salvador offered, grinning. "Steven likes me. Maybe he won't yell at you if I'm along."

I couldn't help smiling. Salvador was right. Steven did like him. And maybe he wouldn't pull my ears off with Salvador there to protect me. I was glad I had someone on my team.

Upstairs, I knocked on Steven's door. There was no answer. "Steven?" I opened the door a crack. He wasn't there.

I backed up and looked down the hallway. The den door was shut. "Steven's probably still in the den, talking to Cathy on the phone."

"Should we wait before we go in his room?"

I shook my head. "No. We'd better hurry up and get some new CDs downstairs before Gel decides to play DJ again."

We went into Steven's room. The door swung closed behind us and shut out the noise from downstairs. The desk lamp was on, and we went over to where Steven kept his CDs in a big plastic bin. Salvador reached in and pulled one out. "This is a nice one. Very calming. In fact, it might even be powerful enough to turn this into a slumber party after all."

I chuckled. "Then it's probably a little too mellow. Let's find something in between."

Outside the window, I heard the crash of a bottle breaking. I went over to the window and looked out at the back patio.

"What's going on?" Salvador asked.

"I can't tell. The light on the desk is causing a glare."

"Here." Salvador turned off the lamp and came to stand beside me. From the darkness of Steven's room we could see the three guys who had come with Gel passing a bottle around and taking swigs. One of them swayed and fell against the other two. We could hear the faint sounds of high, drunken laughter drifting up to the window.

"Oh no!" I groaned. "Now what do I do?"

Salvador looked at me and gave me a crooked smile. "Don't ask me," he said softly. "You're Wonder Girl." His gaze held mine.

Slowly Salvador took his finger and traced the line of my jaw. My heart was pounding.

What's happening? Is he going to kiss me?

I stood there, frozen, until Salvador gently turned my face upward. Then he leaned down, and he *did* kiss me.

For the first time all night, I knew what to do around Salvador.

I kissed him back.

Anna

"Hey, Anna!" Ronald Rheece screeched. "Look at this!" He was balancing a spoon on his nose.

I shook my head. "Ronald, you're scaring me. No more chocolate for you. Ever."

I'd spotted Elizabeth and Salvador across the living room, but then in all the confusion after Jessica got rid of the police, I'd lost them again.

Now I was elbowing my way through the crowd, keeping an eye out for Kristin, Salvador, or Elizabeth. Anybody who seemed friendly.

I didn't see anybody I knew. Suddenly it seemed like everyone except for me and Ronald was from Sweet Valley High. I was starting to feel majorly conspicuous. I decided to check outside again.

I stepped into the dining room. As I passed by a big bowl of pink punch on the table, I spotted an empty liquor bottle. Shakily I poured a little punch into a cup and tasted it. Just as I thought, someone had laced it.

135

I could feel my stomach begin to churn. If the people at this party were drinking, then . . .

. . . I tried not to think about it. But I couldn't push the images away. I pictured my mother's face when she got the phone call. I remembered the scene at the emergency room. The doctors and the police. The sad voices. *"We're so sorry, Mrs. Wang. The driver was drunk. A teenager driving home from a party. He ran the light and . . ."*

I wiped a tear from my cheek and plunged outside, gulping the air. I couldn't start that movie. If I did, I couldn't stop it. I had to push it away. Learn to deal with reality. The reality was that kids drink at parties.

And sometimes they kill people, my mind added.

"Hello, there, pretty girl." One of Gel's friends stepped toward me. He leaned so close, I could smell the liquor on his breath.

"Get away from me," I told him. He tried to grab me, but I was too fast. I ran back into the house. But once I was in the living room, I saw some guy standing there, passing around glasses full of the punch from the table.

Where was Salvador?

I had to find him. I had to get out of there!

Bethel tapped me on the shoulder, and I jumped about a foot in the air. "Anna, would you do me a favor? Jessica says there are more cups upstairs in Elizabeth's room. Do you know where that is?"

I nodded.

"Would you get them and bring them down? Gel's friends used most of the cups for punch, and now we don't have any for sodas."

"Yes. Yes. I'll get them," I promised. I felt like it was a sign or something. If there weren't any cups for sodas, some kids might drink the alcohol. Was this destiny's way of letting me help someone? How ironic that something incredibly simple—like bringing down more cups—might actually keep some-body from getting hurt.

I ran up the stairs and into Elizabeth's room.

The big sack was sitting on her desk. I picked it up, and as I did, I saw something that made me freeze.

Zone, Issue 1.

The 'zine was sitting right there on Elizabeth's desk with *Wonder Girl* splashed all over the front.

Where was my poem? *She just . . . Elizabeth just took it out?* But she said she liked it! A tear trickled down my face and onto the dummy.

Why did she do this? Why?

That poem was for *Tim*.

I grabbed the sack and ran out the door and down the steps. "Here." I thrust the sack into

Bethel's arms. "Here are the . . ." But I couldn't finish my sentence.

"Are you all right?" Bethel asked.

I didn't answer. I just turned and ran out of the door and into the night, tears streaming down my face.

Jessica

"What is that?" Marlon sneered.

Suddenly the sound system had come back on. This time it wasn't heavy metal—it was one of Dad's albums. Chris was playing it on the turntable.

I heard the horrible sound of a needle scratching across vinyl. Where was Elizabeth? If she didn't get down here with some decent CDs, Gel's friends were going to wind up ruining the sound system and the albums.

I looked around for Lacey and spotted her standing in the dining room, sipping a glass of punch. My good mood was beginning to fray a little. If some of the older guys wanted to drink, well, they were underage and that was bad news, but there really wasn't anything I could do to stop them. Hopefully they would know how to avoid getting caught. But if the junior-high kids were going to start drinking, then we were going to be in way major trouble. I was counting on Lacey to help me out.

"Lacey," I said, walking over to her. "Would you do me a favor and tell Gel's friends to stop messing with the sound system?"

Lacey snorted. "I don't *think* so."

What? I looked at her, wide-eyed. *I can't believe this!* Why couldn't she act like a friend for once? Or at least like a decent human being?

Just then Lila wandered by.

"Lila!" I said, rushing over to her. Maybe she had some pull with the high-school crowd. "Help me convince these guys that we need to shut down the music system."

Lila gave me a no-way look. "Are you *kidding?*" she whispered. "Nothing kills a party faster than turning off the music."

I was so surprised that I just stood there a minute. *Isn't Lila going to back me up?* I wondered. I thought she was my *friend.* "Look, Lila, I think this one needs to be murdered," I said.

She shook her head. "Well, don't count on me to be the major dork who lectures these guys on maturity."

Unfortunately Lacey heard that comment and turned slightly, smiling meanly. "You don't need to lecture anyone to look like a dork," she said.

"And you don't need to open your mouth to look like a rude witch," Lila responded coldly. Then she turned to me. "Jessica, would you please tell this—*thing*—to shut her mouth?"

I stared at Lila. Did she really expect me to stand up for her when she wasn't willing to stand up for me?

Lacey looked me in the eye. "Do you have something to say?" she asked.

I shook my head. "No," I said. "I don't."

Lacey smiled, and Lila looked shocked. Who cared? Let them deal with each other.

Just then some of the guys near the sound system began yelling. I almost wished Steven would come downstairs. Should I go get him?

No way. I'd never hear the end of it.

Lila gave me a tight smile. "Looks like things are getting a little out of hand, Jessica," she said. "I think I'll be going." She walked over to Roary, put her arm through his, and signaled to her friends. The next thing I knew, she was trooping out the front door, leaving me with a big mess and a bunch of drunk guys.

Suddenly I felt furious. What had been the point of all this? To impress my friends? *What* friends?

I looked around the living room. Who were these kids? With the exception of Brian, Bethel, Kristin, and a few other people, I didn't even know who they were.

Suddenly the music cranked up full blast.

"*Disco!*" some guy yelled, and then he started

141

scratching the needle back and forth across the record like a funk DJ.

It was my dad's very favorite record. The one that some rock star autographed for him when he was in college.

I didn't even stop to think. I just acted. I dove for the cord to the sound system and pulled it out of the wall.

The music stopped.

The guys by the sound system started booing.

"Hey!" Marlon slurred. "What's up?"

Chris swayed and knocked over a chair.

"What's up is that you're out of here," I snapped.

There was dead silence. Not one person said a word. It was so quiet, I could hear my own heart hammering in my chest.

Gel stepped forward. "What did you say?"

"I said you guys will have to leave. Now."

"Ahem!" Lacey slouched into the living room, sipping her drink. "Excuse me, Jessica, but these guys happen to be friends of Gel's. If they leave, he leaves. If he leaves, I leave."

I looked around the room. Kristin stared at the floor. Ditto Bethel and Brian. Okay, so maybe I was overreacting and making a total fool of myself, but I didn't care.

"Thanks for coming," I said levelly. "I'll see you Monday at school."

Lacey gave a little laughing gasp. "Are you serious?"

I nodded slowly, aware that I was probably committing complete social suicide. But I didn't even care. What was the point of being so-called friends with these people? I wanted them out—*all* of them. They didn't care about anybody but themselves. They just wanted to do what they wanted to do—no matter what kind of trouble they caused.

I swallowed and felt ashamed of myself. Was I any different? I'd made all kinds of trouble for Elizabeth, and Steven, and Cathy—just so I could have my party.

Well, maybe it was time to develop a little spine. "I'm really glad you came," I said firmly. "And I'll see you on Monday."

Then I walked over to the front door and opened it.

Lacey looked around and shrugged, as if to say, "What can you do with somebody like this?" and then she walked out. Gel followed.

"Gel!" Danny called, running after him. "I'm all right to drive. Give me the keys."

Gel stared at his friend, and for a minute I was afraid that he was going to refuse. But eventually he just nodded. "Anybody else need a ride?" Danny asked.

There were a few shouts of "Yeah," and then a few of the high-school guys left with Danny.

Ronald trotted after them. "Wait up!" he called. "I need a ride too! Bye, Jessica," he called over his shoulder. "Great party!"

I watched him go, then let out a relieved sigh.

"Jessica!" Aaron Dallas walked over. "It's okay if all of *us* stay and party, right?" He jerked his head in the direction of Todd and a few other SVMSers.

I looked into his eyes. Was he ever my friend either? I was too tired to think about it. "Sorry," I told him. "Party's over. You can stay and help clean up if you want."

He looked surprised—and a little hurt. I knew what he was thinking—that the old Jessica Wakefield never would have thrown people out of a party. That Jessica would have made sure that everyone had a good time until the bitter end. I knew that was what he was thinking because I was thinking the same thing. Sometimes I felt like I didn't know myself anymore.

Finally Aaron frowned. "Let's go, Todd," he called. "Later, Jessica." And they left. So did everyone else from SVMS. Just like that.

My old friends sure didn't have a problem saying good-bye.

Within five minutes the living room was empty with the exception of Bethel, Brian, and Kristin.

I sank down into a chair and put my head on

my knees. "You guys don't have to stay," I said, feeling pretty miserable.

"Hey!" Brain said. "No way am I leaving. There's still a ton of food left."

I lifted my head. I had expected them to despise me for losing my temper and acting like a little kid. But they were looking at me with . . . *admiration.*

Bethel nodded. "Good party, Jessica."

"How can you say that?"

Brain shrugged. "Hey! Where I'm from, it's not a party if the police don't come and you don't have to throw the drunks out."

Everybody laughed. Brian went into the kitchen and came back out with a big garbage bag. "I'll get the cups and plates."

Bethel slapped her hands on her hips. "Well! Where do you keep the vacuum?" she asked in a brisk tone.

I couldn't believe it. "You guys are going to help me clean up?"

"Of course. Cleanup's half the fun," Bethel said.

I didn't even care if she was lying. I just smiled at her and shook my head. "Well, then, you sure came for the right half."

Elizabeth

Finally the kiss ended. We stood there, staring at each other. I guess neither one of us knew what to do—or say. Salvador was a shade of red I can't begin to describe.

"Elizabeth—," he began.

The door flew open. "What are you two doing in here?" Steven demanded.

"Steven!" I said. "We were just—we were just—"

"Getting some music," Salvador finished. He held up a CD as evidence.

"Well, you can forget it," Steven said. "Party's over."

"What?" I asked.

"Party's over," Steven repeated. "Go downstairs and check it out if you don't believe me." Salvador and I looked at each other.

"I guess we should get downstairs anyway," I said.

"Yeah," Salvador agreed softly.

"You should get out of my room is what you should do," Steven put in.

I glared at him as we walked out the door.

Elizabeth

Salvador followed me. I was secretly thrilled that I didn't have to talk to him at that moment. I had no idea what I would say.

When we got downstairs, it was like the twilight zone. There was nobody in the living room except Bethel and Kristin. "What happened?" I asked. "Where is everybody?"

"Brian and Jessica just took some garbage out into the garage," Kristin said.

"I think Elizabeth meant everyone else," Salvador said. "You know. The party."

Bethel rolled her eyes, and Kristin made a drinking motion with her hand. "Gel and his friends started drinking and getting rowdy, so Jessica threw them out," Kristin said.

"Drinking?" Salvador repeated.

"Jessica threw them *out?*" I asked. Wow. This was a *really* weird night.

"Where's Anna?" Salvador asked. His voice sounded strange, and when I looked over at him, I saw that he had gone pale.

"She got upset about something and ran out," Bethel said.

Salvador looked horrified. "What's wrong?" I asked him.

Suddenly Kristin gasped and almost dropped the punch bowl she had been holding. Punch splashed all over her, but she didn't seem to notice.

Kristin turned to Salvador, wide-eyed. "Do you think it was because of—"

"Oh *no*," Bethel said.

Salvador nodded. What were they all talking about? Why did everyone seem to know what was going on except for me?

"What is it?" I asked. "Would somebody please tell me?"

Bethel and Kristin stared at Salvador. "Anna's brother was killed by a drunk driver," he said quietly. "Last year. He was hit by a kid coming home from a party."

My head was spinning. "What?" I asked. *Anna never told me this,* I thought. *Why didn't Anna ever tell me this?*

"It's true," Salvador said, looking me in the eye.

All of a sudden so many things made sense. Anna's poem, for one thing. How could I have been so blind?

"I have to go." Salvador walked to the front door. I hurried after him.

"What should I do?" I asked him in the doorway.

He gave me a sad smile. "There's nothing you can do this time," he said, "Wonder Girl."

Then he was gone.

Wonder Girl. I wished more than anything it were true.

Jessica

Okay, being grounded stinks.

Even though we did a really good job cleaning up, Mom and Dad *freaked* when they found out about the party. Our next-door neighbor called and ratted us out about the noise and the fact that the cops were here. When Dad heard that part, I thought his head was going to explode.

Luckily it didn't. I've spent enough time cleaning up around here.

So now none of us—me, Steven, or Elizabeth—are allowed to go anywhere except to school or to school-related activities. We aren't allowed to talk on the phone unless it's for something school related. We aren't even allowed to watch TV.

It's not even like I can complain to Elizabeth about it—she's too busy moaning about Anna and Salvador and about how she's so confused, blah, blah, blah. But then she refuses to explain what she's talking about.

I still keep thinking about the party. How I

threw all of my old friends out—even Aaron. Part of me can't believe I did that. I guess I've really changed a lot since I've been at this new school.

You know that saying, "You can't go home again"? Well, I always thought that was really stupid. I mean, if you can't go home, where *else* can you go? But now I think I understand what it means. It means that once you've changed, home will look like a different place to you. And maybe it won't be comfortable anymore.

Like how I felt with Lila. And Aaron.

Not that my new home—SVJH—is that much more comfortable. I can live without Lacey Frells in my life, that's for sure.

But the good part is, if this grounding period ever ends, it looks like I'll have friends to hang out with.

Of course, Bethel, Brian, and Kristin aren't the friends I expected to have as a result of this whole party thing.

They're better.